LOVE

www.chellebliss.com

CHELLE BLISS

USA TODAY BESTSELLING AUTHOR

COPYRIGHT

MEN OF INKED SERIES

"One of the sexiest series of all-time"

-Bookbub Reviewers

Download book 1 for FREE!

- Book 1 - Throttle Me (Joe aka City)
- Book 2 - Hook Me (Mike)
- Book 3 - Resist Me (Izzy)
- Book 4 - Uncover Me (Thomas)
- Book 5 - Without Me (Anthony)
- Book 6 - Honor Me (City)
- Book 7 - Worship Me (Izzy)

ALFA INVESTIGATIONS SERIES

Wickedly hot alphas with tons of heart pounding suspense!

- Book 1 - Sinful Intent (Morgan)
- Book 2 - Unlawful Desire (Frisco)
- Book 3 - Wicked Impulse (Bear)
- Book 4 - Guilty Sin (Ret)

MEN OF INKED: SOUTHSIDE SERIES

Join the Chicago Gallo Family with their strong alphas, sassy women, and tons of fun.

- Book 1 - Maneuver (Lucio)
- Book 2 - Flow (Daphne)
- Book 3 - Hook (Angelo)
- Book 4 - Hustle (Vinnie)
- Book 5 - Love (Angelo)

SINGLE READS

- Mend
- Enshrine
- Misadventures of a City Girl
- Misadventures with a Speed Demon
- Rebound (Flash aka Sam)
- Top Bottom Switch (Ret)

NAILED DOWN SERIES

- Book 1 - Nailed Down
- Book 2 - Tied Down
- Book 3 - Kneel Down

TAKEOVER DUET

What happens when you sleep with your biggest enemy?

- Book 1 - Acquisition
- Book 2 - Merger

FILTHY SERIES

- Dirty Work
- Dirty Secret
- Dirty Defiance

LOVE AT LAST SERIES

- Book 1 - Untangle Me
- Book 2 - Kayden

BOX SETS & COLLECTIONS

- Men of Inked Volume 1
- Men of Inked Volume 2
- Love at Last Series
- ALFA Investigations Series
- Filthy Series
- Takeover Duet

View Chelle's entire collection of books at menofinked.com/books

To learn more about Chelle's books visit *menofinked.com* or *chellebliss.com*

PROLOGUE

ANGELO

The only constant in life is time. One second drips into the next, drifting to minutes, hours, days, and so on. The older we grow, the quicker each year passes into an endless blur of memories and moments we can never re-live.

We're powerless to stop the progression of time. Powerless to stave off the moment our life is extinguished and our time in this world comes to an end.

I don't know what comes after we take our final breath. My faith and belief in something more, something bigger, died the same day my Marissa closed her eyes forever. It's hard to believe in something better, something good, when a person you love is ripped from your life in an instant.

Time, even though it moved around me, seemed to stand still. Frozen. Like I was in an endless coma, able to hear and see, but unable to take part or feel anything besides the darkness.

I thought my chance at happiness had passed years ago. I thought my world had ended. The blackness seemed inescapable.

Sure, I appeared okay on the outside. I had two little kids to take care of. Small pieces of my wife that I couldn't ignore. I put on a good face, tried my best not to be an asshole when all I felt was rage and anguish.

But everything changed when I met Tilly. The sweet Southern girl with an infectious laugh and kind smile.

I never thought I could feel this way again. Never thought my heart would race from a single glance or my stomach would flutter after a simple touch.

Tilly chased away the darkness. Made time move forward once more, requiring me to be present. No longer was I stuck, watching the world move around me...

I was finally alive again.

I was present in the moments...big and small.

She didn't just give me love—she gave me life.

CHAPTER ONE

ANGELO

"THIS IS THE LAMEST BACHELOR PARTY *EVER*." Vinnie crushes the beer can in his palm, clearly annoyed and not bothering to hide his feelings either.

I'd gone over this with Vinnie what felt like a million times. I didn't want a bachelor party. I'd had one when I married Marissa, and that was enough. But he whined. Complained he was too young to go out with us then and missed out on something great. So, I agreed to this to make my little brother happy. Plus, anytime I could get everyone together, it was a good thing.

"Shut up." Lucio smacks him on the shoulder before handing him another beer. "Just drink and keep your trap closed. You're such a whiny baby lately."

"You're the one who's soft now." Vinnie slowly shakes his head, popping open the top of the beer. "I never thought I'd see the day your ass would be such a pussy."

I chuckle behind the rim of my drink, trying to hide my laughter at their stupidity. They are both pussy-whipped. Hell, so am I, but I don't try to hide the fact like they do.

Lucio barks out a laugh. "That's priceless coming from you. Bianca has you completely by the short hairs."

Vinnie's eyes darken. "She does not." He takes a swig of his beer before wiping his lips with the back of his hand. "Fuck." He grimaces. "Maybe she does. What the hell happened to us?" he asks, looking around the table as we wait for the rest of the party-goers to get here.

I can't wipe the stupid smirk off my face. Vinnie and Lucio used to bust my balls about Marissa. For years, I listened to their bullshit and their promises that they'd never fall so deep that they'd settle down and become domesticated like I had been.

"It's love," Leo says before bringing his glass of

bourbon to his lips. "Love does funny shit to our heads."

Ah, Leo. He's a man of few words. He's usually quiet around the family, probably still feeling like an outsider most of the time. The checkered past between our fathers clouds everything, including his ability to open up and feel like he's one of us. Slowly, the wall he'd built has been crumbling, though. It doesn't hurt that Daphne is such a ballbuster, telling him to get over his shit because everyone else had long ago.

"No." Vinnie swipes his thumb across the water droplets running down the can. "That's our dick. That's where love starts."

My little brother looks at the world very differently from the rest of us. Of course, he'd think love started in his dick. Everything centered around his cock. *Everything.*

"Love starts in our dicks?" Lucio raises an eyebrow and stares at Vinnie in disbelief.

Vinnie runs his fingers through his thick brown hair and sighs. "Of course, moron. You don't fall in love with a chick unless she gives you a hard-on. Ya know? She has to give you feels here—" he grabs his crotch, and then he slides his hand to his chest "—before you feel it here."

Everyone at the table laughs. I'm not laughing at

his words, because there's truth in them; I'm laughing because my brother is talking about love.

I never thought I'd see the day when he'd even consider settling down, but now he's engaged with a baby on the way, even if he's been great at hiding the pregnancy.

I knew the signs. The biggest one was that Bianca stopped drinking when she came to the bar right around the same time they announced their engagement. Hello. That's the biggest clue ever. No one stops drinking all of a sudden unless they're ill, pregnant, or gave up alcohol for Lent.

Her body's changed some in the last few months, just like Marissa's did when she was pregnant with Tate and Brax.

"Well..." Lucio pauses for a moment as he stares down at his beer. "I never thought about it that way."

"It's not until you're balls deep into a chick and she's moaning your name that you think—" Vinnie spreads his arms out, becoming more animated "—fuck, I think I'm in love."

"You're so romantic," Leo mutters against the glass and peers at him over the rim.

"You ever loved someone you haven't fucked, Leo?" Vinnie winces as soon as the words are out of his mouth.

The realization that he's talking about our sister must've finally smacked him in that stupid head of his.

"Have you ever loved someone you weren't attracted to?" He corrects himself because none of us can stomach the thought of Daphne fucking anyone, even her husband.

Leo shakes his head. "I've only loved one person in my life."

"Loved?" I ask, catching his words and totally fucking with him because it's so damn easy.

"You know what the hell I mean. Jesus, asshole. I'm head over heels for the crazy woman. I could never love anyone, beautiful or not, the way I love her."

I knew his words were true. The man put his life on the line to be with Daphne. I don't know many men who would go to that length to be with a woman. That's when I knew he was truly in love with my sister. For that, he's earned my respect.

"I don't know how you put up with her shit all the time. She's the biggest ballbuster." Lucio lifts his beer to Leo. "You deserve a Husband of the Year award or some shit."

"I wouldn't have your sister any other way."

They say there's someone for everyone, and I'd say they're right because there aren't many men in the world who can put up with Daphne's dramatics, bossiness, and overall pain-in-the-assness.

"Even when she's being..." Vinnie's voice trails off for a moment, and I can tell he's choosing his words wisely for once.

"Don't finish that statement," Leo warns.

He's always protective of his wife, even when it comes to us.

"Where the fuck are they?" Vinnie asks, being smart and changing the subject to something that isn't going to get Leo all riled up.

I lean back, glancing at my watch. "The plane landed an hour ago. They had to drop the women off at my place, take the kids, along with Uncle Sal and Aunt Mar, to the hotel before meeting up with us."

"Maybe they aren't coming." Vinnie shrugs, looking toward the doorway. "We can always go without them."

"They're coming," I tell him because I'm not leaving without them.

The "they" we're referring to are our cousins from Florida. This is the first time in years the entire Gallo gang will be back together since they couldn't all make it for Lucio's wedding.

They used to be part of our everyday lives until my uncle Sal uprooted his family and took off for the sun and sand in the South.

I wonder sometimes how life would've been different if they'd stuck around. I'd always been close with my cousins, but we were constantly getting into trouble. I'm sure that had something to do with the move, along with his utter disgust for my father and his inability to keep the family name out of the newspaper.

Before Vinnie can complain again, the door to the bar swings open and the motley crew walks inside.

"Honey, we're home," Mike announces, standing tall and towering over everyone else.

He looks good, better than I remember the last time I saw him. Even though he's given up fighting in the ring, he's kept in shape and is as big as ever.

I followed his fighting career as best I could. Our fathers weren't speaking at the time, but that didn't mean I didn't want my cousin to achieve greatness. And he did too. He won a title, got married, and popped out a few kids. He looked happy. Content. I knew that look because I'd been sporting it too with Tilly.

Lucio's the first to stand, stalking toward my cousins with open arms. "You fuckers. I wasn't sure you'd show your ugly mugs."

"Get the fuck outta here." Joe waves my brother off as Lucio tries to hug him. "We weren't missing this for anything in the world."

Joe never seems to age, and his edge never fades. The man has always been intense, more intense than me, which is saying something. His dark hair has splashes of gray near the temples, no doubt caused by having daughters on the verge of dating.

Vinnie's on his feet and next to Lucio within seconds, excited to meet the cousins he'd been too young to hang out with. "Hey," Vinnie says with a chin lift, always trying to be the cool bastard in the room.

"There he is," Mike says as he steps forward and grabs Vinnie, lifting him off the floor like he isn't freakishly large. "You little asshole went and became a badass football player and shit."

Mike was always the silly one. We'd laugh at him until we couldn't breathe. He was such a dork and a complete ass-kisser. Color us shocked when he grew up, filled out, and eventually became a champion fighter. That's the day we all stopped laughing.

"Fuck, man, I can't breathe," Vinnie grits out, trying to break free of Mike's bear hug, but Mike isn't having any of it.

It's funny to see someone as big, if not bigger, than Vinnie holding him like he's a rag doll. By the time the kid turned sixteen, none of us could do shit to him physically because he grew at a freakishly fast rate.

Mike squeezes him tighter, lifting him higher, ignoring Vinnie's whining. "Pussy," he mumbles before he places Vinnie's feet back on the floor.

"Fuck off." Vinnie punches him square in the shoulder.

Mike barely flinches, but he looks down to where Vinnie's hand touched him, then stares at my brother. "Was that supposed to hurt or something?"

"Are you two ladies done?" Lucio asks, taunting them. "Or do you need more time to hug it out and shit?"

Thomas pulls up a chair and reaches for an empty glass and the bottle of whiskey. "Longest plane ride of my life," he groans and looks over at James.

"The way the kids bicker, you'd think they were all brothers and sisters," James adds, sitting down next to his brother-in-law and pushing another empty glass toward Thomas, wanting a drink and clearly in need of one. "My ears are still ringing from all that whining."

James and Thomas have a solid bond. More like natural brothers than legally by marriage. It comes from their time working together undercover at the DEA and then opening their own private investigation firm. They're both pretty badass and not anyone I'd fuck with even if they weren't related to me.

"Did you ever think we'd be here?" I ask, looking around the room at the men before me. "I sure as fuck didn't."

We were such shitheads when we were young. Out of control, really. Even though we were younger than them, that didn't stop the antics and shit we pulled. We weren't sitting inside playing Legos or building forts.

Nah. That wasn't our style. We were city kids. Hood rats. We played in the alleys, getting dirt under our fingernails.

"I wasn't sure any of us would make it to this age." Joe pulls a chair across the floor, making the most horrendous noise, before he turns it around and straddles the back. "We did some dumb shit."

"Not me," Mike says, which is technically true. He didn't get into the kind of trouble the rest of us did because he was too busy with sports to give a flying fuck about playing with us. "I was too busy."

Anthony rolls his eyes. "You were always a suck-up. Still are. You didn't want Ma and Pop to think differently of you. Always thought you were better than us."

I'm still amazed Anthony settled down, joining adulthood, and quit his rock band. The man swore he was going to be famous someday and have an unlimited supply of pussy at his disposal. He and Vinnie are so alike in that way, but here they are, taken and one-woman men.

Mike waves his hand in the air. "I am," he answers flatly. "I can't help that I'm pure perfection."

Thomas drags a hand down his face, muttering something into his palm. "Anyway, are we just chilling here for the night?"

Vinnie shakes his head. "Nope. I made all the plans. Our ride will be here in ten." He smiles.

I pinch the bridge of my nose, wishing I'd called this off weeks ago. The last thing I want to do is party my ass off the night before my wedding. I don't give two fucks about drinking, strip clubs, or whatever insanity Vinnie has planned. And I know there will be insanity.

"Where are we going?" My voice comes out harsher than I'd planned, but I plaster a smile across my face instead of grimacing in an attempt not to come off as a complete asshole.

"Well..." Vinnie clears his throat, and I brace myself. "I know you don't want to go to the strip club."

"No," I blurt out. "I have the only tits I ever want to see at home."

"Amen," Joe agrees as his brothers and mine nod their heads in agreement.

"Yeah, Bianca would have my balls anyway." Vinnie glances toward the ceiling and sighs.

"Already does," Lucio mutters under his breath so quietly, Vinnie doesn't hear.

Thank fuck.

"I made reservations at the best steakhouse in town, and then we're going to a gentlemen's club."

"Dude, I said no strip clubs," I remind him,

grinding my teeth together to stop myself from yelling at him.

He shakes his head quickly. "I know, fucker. It's not that kind of 'gentlemen's club.'" He uses air quotes on the last two words. "It's truly a club for men only. We can play cards, hang out and smoke cigars, or whatever the fuck we want to do without having to worry about women bothering us."

The Vinnie from a year ago wouldn't have worried about attention from women. He never would've made a plan that involved only men. Never. But that's what love does. For once, he's no longer thinking with his dick, even though that's where his love apparently started.

I slowly shake my head. "You really are whipped, huh?"

My statement earns me a middle finger. "You can fuck right off. Every guy around this table is whipped in some fashion."

"Unless you're like James," Morgan says with a bit of laughter.

I've missed Morgan.

I remember the day he left for boot camp, waving to us over his shoulder as he walked inside the hotel, ready to join the army. Aunt Fran couldn't bear to take him herself, and instead of my mother going alone with her, she piled us into the car to wish our cousin farewell. Never did I think he wouldn't come back. I always thought he'd be a Southsider again and come back into the fold. The guy had a restless spirit, though, especially after he was a SEAL.

James throws up his hands. "Oh, no. Don't think I'm the boss all the time. Izzy can hold her own."

"Uh-huh." Anthony laughs and rubs his chin, eyeing his brother-in-law. "You let her whip your ass too? Or does she put you over her knee and spank you?"

I lean back in my seat, waiting for the fireworks to fly, or more likely, fists, as James's eyes darken and focus on Anthony.

"Oh." Vinnie moves his chair a little closer to the table. "You two get down like that?" He waggles his eyebrows, totally amused.

James tips his chin up, turning to Vinnie across the table with a completely straight and unreadable face. "Why don't you ask her? I'm sure she'd be more than happy to answer."

"James, are you trying to end his pro career before he's really had a chance to get started?" Thomas presses his fingers against his temples. "I swear to fuck, Izzy will eat him for dinner."

Vinnie chuckles. "Izzy's a little thing, isn't she? I think I can hold my own."

Laughter erupts around the table because everyone

knows Izzy's trouble with a capital T. She may look small, but fuck, not even I would mess with her.

"Then ask her," James tells Vinnie with a smirk.

"Fuck." Vinnie runs his hand back through his hair and nods, playing it cool. "I will, man."

"Don't." I place my hand on Vinnie's arm. "Don't fuck with Izzy. Like, for real. If you like your balls in any way, don't say shit to her."

"Come on." Vinnie doesn't look convinced. "I've put up with Daphne for years."

"Daphne's a cream puff compared to Izzy, kid. Don't fuck with her, or you'll get bit," Joe tells Vinnie, pointing his finger at him to drive the point home. "I'm dead serious. We taught her to fight—and I don't mean like a girl. She's South Side one hundred percent. She will not hesitate to kick your ass."

"Our ride is here," Lucio says, ticking his chin toward the doorway and climbing quickly to his feet. "Let's get a move on. I'm starving."

"Roger's meeting us later. He had to stay at the office late," Vinnie says, jamming his phone into his pocket as he heads toward the door.

"Good," I say. I'm happy my soon-to-be brother-in-law will be joining us. Technically, he's not my brother-in-law at all, but what else would I call him? He's like a brother to Tilly, the only other family besides us she has. Therefore, he's one of us too.

I lock up the bar as the guys pile into the party bus. I'm happy we decided to close down for a few nights to celebrate, opting to spend time with the family over anything else.

In the end, that's all we have anyway.

Money isn't important, things are irrelevant, but family is the only other constant besides time.

CHAPTER TWO

TILLY

Betty's taken the kids for the night. She said I needed a girls' night out before the *big day*. I told her I didn't want to go out, and I'd rather be home with Brax and Tate than anywhere else in the world.

She wouldn't hear it.

"Trust me, sweetheart. You'll thank me someday," she said when she picked them up. "Your cousins will be here soon to get you."

Cousins? No one said anything about meeting the cousins tonight. I figured I'd hang out with Daphne, Bianca, and Delilah for the night, drinking a few martinis and laughing about our crazy men.

Clearly, they had other plans and didn't bother to share them with me.

I knew the guys were all together, and I should've known the women would be too. I begged them not to make a big deal out of tonight. It is my second marriage, after all, and I'm not a young kid, looking to party and get drunk, having my final night of freedom.

I'd been alone long enough.

I'm getting married tomorrow.

I repeat the words over and over in my head as I change my clothes, fix my makeup, and pull my hair into a tight ponytail. The entire thing still feels surreal. I never thought I'd walk down the aisle again. Figured I'd be alone forever because moving on was too painful and the memory of Mitchell haunted me sometimes too.

But then Angelo happened.

That man, with his fine ass, sweet lips, and rough hands, swept me off my feet, not giving me a chance to catch my breath. The kids just sealed the deal. Especially Tate. That little girl had me wrapped around her finger from the moment I met her. She knew it too, using my feelings for her to her advantage, but I didn't mind.

The door opens downstairs as I smooth out the top of my hair, and my fingers begin to tremble, almost ruining my updo. I push away the panic and take a deep breath, looking at myself in the mirror one last time.

"You can do this," I tell myself, like I need a pep talk to be around people.

I've always been a people person, but there's something so intimidating about the fact that I'm meeting his family. My family.

Holy shit.

Not only am I marrying a man, but his entire, huge-ass Italian family comes as part of the package. The thought is overwhelming after being along for so very long.

"Tilly! Where the hell are you, girl?" Daphne yells up the stairway as I'm still trying to pull on my strappy sandals, but they're not cooperating.

"Coming!" I yell back, hopping on one foot, trying like hell not to fall over. I catch myself on the edge of the bed and sit quickly, somehow getting my sandals on with my shaking fingers.

I take a deep breath as I climb to my feet and go to the full-length mirror near the closet. I look good. No, I look damn good. I only wish Angelo could see me looking this fabulous, rocking my sexy outfit and with my hair up the way he likes it.

"It'll be okay," I say to my reflection before I take off toward the hallway. As I make my way downstairs, I see them all gathered in the foyer, talking and laughing, but they're not looking at me.

"There she is," Daphne says, meeting my eyes and waving her hand in my direction.

Everyone turns to look at me, and I feel the flush across my face. "Hi," I squeak, unable to play it cool.

Shit.

They're all beautiful. I should've known. They are Gallos, after all. Or at least married to one. I don't mean cute or a little pretty but drop-dead gorgeous.

"This is Mia, Max, Izzy, Race, Angel, and Suzy," Daphne rattles off, pointing to each one as she says their name.

I wave, not bothering to talk because I don't want to sound like a tween girl.

Daphne grabs my hand as soon as I'm close enough and pulls me to her. "Isn't she perfect?"

I don't know what to do or how to act as they all just stare at me. This must be what it's like to be a zoo animal. "Oh, stop," I say with a hint of laughter.

"I can see why Angelo's head over heels for you," a woman says, pushing her dark hair off her shoulders. "You have the sweet, innocent thing nailed like our Suzy." She turns to the blond woman standing behind her. "Isn't that right, Sunshine?"

"Izzy, you know I'm not innocent, and I'm sure as hell not sweet anymore."

Okay. So, the sassy one is Izzy. Angelo clued me in about his little cousin and how she's a spitfire and one hundred percent trouble. He said she was like Daphne, but scarier, and doesn't put up with anyone's shit.

Then there's Suzy, who Izzy calls Sunshine. She does look sweet and innocent, but I know she's married to Angelo's cousin Joe, and I've been told he's pretty badass, covered in tattoos, and drives a Harley.

Izzy laughs loudly. "You're a complete whore, but I remember when you weren't so easy."

"Oh, shut up. I'm not easy," Suzy snaps back.

"Did you or did you not sleep with my brother the night you met him?" Izzy stares at Suzy with a small smirk playing on her lips.

I widen my eyes. I don't know if I should take cover or stay still because I'm pretty sure there's about to be fireworks.

"He was just so damn hot on that bike, and I was drunk—"

"You were as sober as they come," Izzy interrupts. "Don't lie."

Suzy pulls her white cardigan tighter around her body and squares her shoulders. "Um, if I remember right, you slept with James the night you met him too."

"I was drunk." Izzy waves her off.

"Pot meet kettle," a woman with long wavy hair

and olive skin says, pushing them both aside. "I'm Mia, Mike's wife."

Mike is the championship fighter. I've seen pictures of him, and he's enormous but has the kindest smile.

"Oh, sweet Jesus. I'm not defining myself by a man, even my man. I'm Max," the woman at her side says.

"It's lovely to meet you," I say, trying not to run upstairs and barricade myself in our room.

"Anthony's wife," Daphne whispers in my ear, which earns her an eyebrow raise from Max because she wasn't super quiet about it.

This is so overwhelming. More than I thought it would be. I know I should be a little more outgoing. Hell, they aren't holding back. But I can't seem to stop myself from digging my fingernails into my palm to settle my ass down.

"Shall we go?" Daphne asks, ticking her head toward the door. "The limo is waiting."

"Limo?" My mouth falls open because I've never been in a limo.

I suddenly feel lame because I'm the only one in the room that seems even remotely excited about this.

Daphne nods. "Well, yeah. We're getting shit-faced, and we needed a designated driver. None of these bitches was going to stay sober." She pitches her finger over her shoulder toward everyone. "So, we have a driver and a city waiting for us."

"Nothing too crazy, right?" I raise an eyebrow at my soon-to-be sister-in-law because I know how she is.

"Of course," she scoffs like it's absolutely absurd of me to think she had something risqué planned.

"There better be at least a naked chest somewhere," the redhead says, blushing a little bit when Suzy smacks her arm.

"Tonight's like Vegas. What happens tonight stays between us. Got me?" Daphne narrows her eyes as she looks around at her cousins. "I mean it. No pictures. No videos. No memories. No evidence."

"I like the way you think." Izzy smirks.

Suzy rolls her eyes, but the rest of the group is nodding along. I know we're in trouble. The night isn't going to be a girls' night at the spa or sipping wine at some dark, cozy bar.

Nope.

"Where are we going?" I ask as I pull the front door closed, making sure it's locked before following behind them toward the waiting limo.

"First stop is Gavin's for some martinis, then we have tickets to a show," Daphne says over her shoulder.

"What kind of show?" My stomach flips a little because Daphne's looking at me in such a way that I know she isn't telling me everything.

"It's like the ballet."

"Like the ballet?" I ask flatly.

She nods quickly and hooks her arm with mine, leading me toward the sleek black limo. "There're men dancing."

I stop walking. "I said no strippers."

"You said no penis." She giggles. "They'll have on bottoms. Don't worry so much." She pulls on my arm, trying to get me to move, but I don't.

"Daphne." My voice is laced with agitation because she didn't listen to me at all. I don't know why I thought she would. Daphne always does what Daphne wants to do.

"We'll take a vote over drinks, okay? Majority wins."

I think about her words for a moment, wondering if I'm being overly sensitive. I don't want to ruin the evening for everyone. They've come so far for my wedding, and the last thing I want to do is be the one to nix the entire evening. I am not Tilly the Party Pooper. I never wanted to be that girl.

"When did you become such a prude?" she asks, knowing full well I'm not.

"I'm not a prude," I huff out, completely annoyed.

She tilts her head, smirking at me. "So totally are. It's not like they're going to be waving their dicks in your face. It's just some naked chest, for shit's sake."

Part of me knows she's right. The club is public, so it's not like anything salacious will happen, but there's still a part of me that's completely uncomfortable with seeing another man half undressed and him throwing his junk in my face.

"Does your brother know?" I raise an eyebrow.

"Of course," she says, but her eyes don't meet mine.

I cross my arms over my chest as the girls inside the limo gawk at us. "He does?"

"Yes. He wasn't exactly thrilled about the idea, but I promised him nothing over the top would happen."

"No lap dances," I tell her, narrowing my eyes.

She practically breaks out into a happy dance at my words. "Deal," she squeals before turning to the girls and raising her arms in triumph. "Drinks and dicks, bitches."

An hour later and two martinis down, my head's already buzzing from the alcohol. The last thing I want to do tonight is get drunk. I don't want to walk down the aisle with a hangover, barely able to focus on the man waiting at the altar for me.

"Another?" Max asks, tipping her head toward my empty glass.

I shake my head, trying to pace myself. These girls, the cousins and my soon-to-be sisters-in-law, sure can toss the drinks back without seeming to be affected by them. "I better slow down a little," I say, slurring the last word a bit before breaking out into a fit of giggles.

"She's cut off," Izzy, whom I've realized is bossier than Daphne, says and shakes her fingers. "We can't get her drunk."

"Thank fuck you have a late wedding." Delilah lifts her glass to her lips and stares at me from across the table. "I'd hate to be up at the ass-crack of dawn to get my hair done."

I laugh at the word ass-crack, and I know I'm half in the bag. Liquor doesn't usually have this much of an effect on me, but I hadn't eaten much today, trying to fit into my already tight wedding gown tomorrow.

"What's so funny?" Delilah stares at me, moving her glass around the tabletop in small little circles.

"You said ass-crack," I blurt out before laughing louder, even snorting a little.

"I agree. She's cut off," Mia says quickly. "Let her sober up a little before you order her another one."

I roll my eyes. "Is there a Gallo who isn't bossy?"

"Nope," Angel replies. "They're all a pain in the ass, especially the men."

Max swats Angel on the arm with the back of her hand. "Girl, Thomas is a walk in the park compared to Anthony."

"I win the award for most controlling husband."

Izzy lifts her hands in the air and points down at herself. "Your men are all a walk in the park."

Suzy, the cute perky blonde, gawks at Izzy. "You think Joe's easy?" She laughs loudly and slaps the table. "Oh, James, spank me," she teases, leaning forward and wiggling her ass a little bit for effect.

Izzy shakes her head. "That's not how I say it, and you know it."

Suzy clears her throat. "You're right. It's more like 'Spank me, Sir.'" Then she pauses as Izzy stares at her over the rim of her martini glass. "Do you use Sir or Master?"

I raise my eyebrows. This is an interesting turn of events, and suddenly my laughter dies and I'm pulled into their conversation.

"It depends on my mood." Izzy shrugs.

"Bullshit," Max coughs and covers her mouth, hiding her amusement.

Izzy places her glass on the table, letting her hand slide down the stem. "What's bullshit?"

"It depends on what he *allows* you to call him," Max says with a crooked smirk.

"Oh." Bianca suddenly becomes interested in the conversation and turns toward Izzy. "He's a Dom?"

"You know about the lifestyle?"

Bianca waves. "Romance writer and I thoroughly research my books. Thoroughly," she repeats with a huskier voice. "I know all about the lifestyle or, at least, as much as I can read about it."

"Ever been to a club, kid?" Izzy asks.

Bianca shakes her head. "No, but I've done a lot of reading."

"They're hot," Suzy says, surprising me because she seems too innocent to even know what the hell they're talking about.

"You've been?" I ask, and my mouth suddenly feels drier than the desert.

Suzy nods as a blush creeps into her cheeks, clearly visible in the shitty lighting because her skin is so pale.

"Chicago has one of the best clubs," Izzy tells Bianca. "If you ever want to do research the right way, I can get you in."

Bianca swallows hard and places her hand on her chest. "You could do that?"

Izzy nods. "I know the owner pretty well. James has been his friend for years."

"Vinnie wouldn't like that too much," Bianca says and blows out a harsh breath.

"Bring him. He'll like it plenty." Izzy laughs. "We all have a bit of voyeur in us."

"Those clubs are real?" I ask Izzy, figuring they were made up, much like most things in fiction.

"They sure as fuck are."

I can't imagine having sex with Angelo in public.

Nor can I imagine watching other people have sex as we watched them. I'm not a complete prude, Angelo makes sure of that, but that doesn't mean I want to share my goods with the world.

"Huh," I mumble.

"I'll give you ladies a choice." She scoots her chair closer to the table, closing the space between us. "We can go to the strip show or the club. Which is it?"

Mia sways backward. "You can get us in? I mean, Mike would fucking have my head."

"They have a viewing room on the second level. You can't interact with anyone, but you can watch what happens in the common areas."

I'm suddenly speechless. I didn't want to do the whole stripper thing, but not because I was worried about Angelo. He trusts me, and I trust him implicitly. But the thought of going somewhere like a sex club, where people may openly be having sex might be stepping over the line. The man is easygoing, but everyone has their breaking point.

"Club," Suzy blurts out.

"Strippers," Max says.

"Club." Bianca nods with a wink at Suzy.

"Club," Mia votes.

"Neither," I say, which earns me a groan and a few straws thrown in my direction followed by the words "party pooper."

We go around the table until it's left up to Izzy to make the final call. Izzy rubs the back of her neck and doesn't speak for a moment. "God, this decision is so hard. The club is more private."

I don't know why that makes me giggle. What's private about a sex club? Her words strike me as odd, and my laughter earns me a look so serious, I instantly sober up.

"I'd have the room cleared so no one else but us would be there. We wouldn't have to worry about anyone bothering us." She taps her fingernail against her lip and glances up at the ceiling. "Strippers can be fun, though, too, but they're so touchy sometimes."

"No one's touching me." Suzy winces. "All those sweaty bodies. Blech."

"I'm with Suzy," I say, because the last thing I want is a man sweating all over me, especially if he's not Angelo. "I told you, no strippers."

Daphne laughs and waves me off. "Fine, it's settled, then. We'll go to the club. Just please say they serve drinks and I have a chance at seeing dick."

Izzy pulls her phone out of her pocket and stares Daphne right in the eye. "Girl, you're going to see more than dick. Just you wait."

I'm suddenly more nervous than I was before the girls arrived. I wanted a quiet night out. An evening with the girls, a few drinks, and nothing more. I never thought the night would turn out this way, and I only pray Angelo won't throw a shit fit when he finds out.

"I'll call Slate and get everything set," Izzy says as she types away on her phone.

"Slate?" I ask. "Is that really his name?" My giggles are back, and the martini I polished off a few minutes ago is finally starting to kick in.

"Fuck if I know." She shrugs. "It's what we call him, though. He's hot as fuck too."

"James will murder you," Angel warns.

"Oh. James can go fuck himself."

There's a collective gasp around the table. Even I make the noise, and I've never even met the man.

"If I'm lucky, I might get an ass-beating tonight." Izzy laughs softly as she continues typing on the small screen. When no one says anything, she looks up. "What?" she asks with her eyebrows drawn down. "Don't knock it until you try it." She pitches her thumb toward Suzy. "This little princess likes her ass spanked too. I know how crazy y'all are in the bedroom, so don't even pretend to act otherwise."

There's laughter around the table, myself included, but I don't know why I'm joining in. I would never call my sex life freaky. It's perfect in every way, but there's nothing about it that makes me think we're doing anything outside the norm.

"Slate?" Izzy says into the phone and covers her

other ear with her hand because Gavin's is loud, almost too loud to hear one another over the music. "It's Izzy Caldo, James's wife." She excuses herself, rushing toward the front door and leaving us behind.

"So, we're doing this?" I ask, swallowing the fear of the unknown.

"It'll be fun," Bianca says and downs the last of her water. "Just relax. What could possibly go wrong?"

CHAPTER THREE

ANGELO

I push my plate away, enjoying the company and the meal, and lean back in my chair. Everyone's talking, catching up after not seeing one another for years. The evening has been great. More than that, it's been like being home again.

"You okay?" Joe asks, leaning over and speaking softly so no one else can hear.

I nod and stare at my cousin, letting a smile spread across my face. "Of course. Tonight's been great."

"Something's eating you," he replies.

I sigh. "Not really. I just never thought I'd be doing

this again. I mean, I'm glad I am. No one wants to be alone, and it's not like we had a choice, but damn..."

He rests his hand on my shoulder. "Everything will be fine, Angelo. I can't imagine everything you've been through, but you deserve some damn happiness."

Marissa's been on my mind a lot lately. The closer we get to the wedding date, the more I think about her. I no longer feel like I'm cheating or betraying our vows, but I wish I could talk to her at least one more time. I wonder what she'd say about Tilly, about the life she and I are building together.

"What's wrong? Lucio asks, staring at Joe and me from across the table. "Are you okay?"

"I'm fine. Couldn't be better." I wave him off.

"You've got to be shitting me," James says while staring down at his phone. "These ladies are seriously trying to kill us tonight."

"What's wrong?" Thomas drops his fork to the table.

"They're going to the Black Door." James runs his hand down his face and groans. "Nothing good can come from this."

"What the hell is the Black Door?" I ask.

"A sex club." Vinnie smirks. "A sexy as fuck one too."

"I don't know what the hell you're smiling about, moron. Bianca's with them," Lucio reminds him.

"Fuck," he hisses and leans back in his chair with all the happiness completely wiped clear of his face. "What the hell are they going to do at a sex club?"

"Give me a minute. Let me make a call," James says and excuses himself from the table, taking his phone with him.

"You've been there?" I ask Vinnie, but it shouldn't surprise me when he nods.

"Of course. I know every place in this godforsaken town. There's no way I want Bianca to go there, though."

I don't want Tilly to go there either. Well, at least not without me there to make sure no crazy-ass shit goes down.

"They seriously try to kill us on the daily when they're all together." Anthony takes another bite of his steak and moans. "This is so fucking good."

"Doesn't it bother you that they're going there?" Vinnie asks Anthony, who doesn't seem to be fazed by the news.

He waves his fork around, chewing. "Yes, but I trust Max. Plus, I know if anyone fucks with her, she will literally claw their eyes out."

James sits back down and shakes his head. "They reserved the VIP viewing room."

"And?" Lucio asks because he's just as fucking clueless as me.

"They'll be alone and only able to watch what's happening while they have drinks."

"So, they're going to watch other people have sex?" Lucio raises an eyebrow.

James nods. "Pretty much. They're not members, so they can't enter the club. But Izzy being Izzy, pulled a few strings and got them access to the viewing room so they can watch the action."

"What time are they going?" Thomas asks as he drops his napkin on his plate and clenches his fist tightly.

"In an hour," James tells him. "Why, you want to crash their little party?" James looks amused by the idea, and I'm not sure how I feel about it.

I don't care what Tilly's doing. As long as she's having a good time, I know everything will be fine. I'm secure in my manhood, and I know my girl. She's a wild thing in the sack, but she's also as loyal as they come.

"Fuck yeah, we're going," Mike barks. "We can't leave them alone. I mean, come on. It could lead to a fun night, too. I'm sure they'll be turned on and..." His voice drifts off.

"We're going," Joe tells everyone. "Give them a little bit of time alone there, and then we'll crash their party."

"You're so calm about this," I tell him, surprised at my cousin.

He shrugs. "We've been to one before in Florida with James and Izzy. Suzy's a curious little thing. She acts all innocent and sweet, but that girl..." He shakes his head and laughs, not finishing his sentence.

"It's settled, then. We're going," Thomas states, making the decision for us.

"Another round," Morgan says to the waiter as he passes by. "We're going to need it."

I'm sure one drink is going to be enough. My girl is going to a sex club. She is going to watch other people having sex, and I know my girl; this is way out of her comfort zone.

A little over an hour later, we're packed inside the party bus, heading toward the Black Door. No one's drunk, but the drinks are still flowing and going down easy while we sit in the nonstop traffic of downtown Chicago.

"Should we tell them we're coming?" Lucio asks, which earns him a glare from James.

"Absolutely not." James shakes his head.

I think about adding my two cents, telling them we should just leave the ladies alone and let them have their fun, but I hold my tongue.

"They need a little surprise. Anyway, I'm pretty

sure the ladies will be in need of us once we arrive," Joe says. "It's pretty intense."

"I just can't picture Tilly there," I mumble, thinking no one's heard me.

Joe nudges me with his elbow, smiling at me. "Suzy isn't a sex club girl, but she's not above watching. There's something intriguing about it. You'll see."

"It's hot as fuck," Vinnie adds as he rubs his hands together, leaning over his legs with his elbows resting on his knees. "So freaking hot."

I try to picture Tilly, sitting somewhere and watching perfect strangers having sex. But for some reason, I can't, no matter how hard I try. There's just something so prim and proper about her, even though she's a freak in the sheets.

Suddenly, a wave of guilt comes over me. This is supposed to be her night to cut loose, have fun with my cousins, and here we are, ready to crash their party.

"Maybe we should leave them be," I say. "Let them have a good time."

That statement earns me an icy stare from James. "I don't know about you, but I don't like the idea of my wife at a sex club without me there to protect her."

"Protect her from what?" I ask, because I have no idea what they're even getting themselves into.

"From anything. This isn't like going to a strip club

where there are rules. If Izzy charms her way into the members-only section..." His voice trails off.

I throw up my hands, giving in. "You know best."

"I know the owner. He'll make sure they're safe, but I'll feel better if we're there, watching them," James tells me.

"Izzy's okay with you just showing up randomly?" Lucio asks.

James's entire demeanor changes as he starts to laugh. "I don't need Izzy's permission to show up anywhere, especially when she uses my name to pull some strings. She knew what she was doing when she placed that call. I'm pretty sure she knows I'll be coming after her, too."

"You make her sound like prey," I say.

He narrows his dark eyes. "She's my wife and my submissive. She knows better than to go to a place like that without me."

My eyebrows rise at his statement. *Submissive?* My cousin submits to a man, even though he's her husband? Izzy is the last person I'd ever think would bow or kneel to anyone.

"We're here." Vinnie tips his head toward a large building right outside the van.

I turn and look over the gray stone exterior with two very large black doors in front. There's no sign with the club name and nothing telling anyone what lies on the other side of the doors.

"Don't let it fool you." Vinnie stands. "What lies behind those doors is absolutely fucking mind-blowing."

"Exactly how many times have you been here?" Leo asks Vinnie as they step off the bus.

Vinnie shrugs. "A few times," he says, being cagey and more like his old self. "You?"

"A couple," Leo says, which surprises me for some reason. "But never with your sister."

Nothing should surprise me anymore, especially when it comes to the men in my life. I was too busy being a dad, working, and then dealing with Marissa's illness to bother with sex clubs.

"Am I the only one who's never been to a place like this?" I ask.

Lucio looks over at me as we step onto the side-walk. "I haven't, and I thought I'd experienced just about everything."

The doors creak loudly as we step into the dark reception area. The music's loud enough that the small decorations in the room bounce and vibrate on their own.

A man dressed in black leather pants and a black tank steps around a tall desk, holding out his hand to

James. "It's been a long time, man. Looking good as ever, and so is that pretty little wife of yours."

James shakes the man's hand, but there's no joy on his face. "Slate. Are they up there?"

Slate's eyes rise toward a staircase to the second level. "Alone, just as I promised they'd be."

"You should've told her no," James says, and I can hear the annoyance in his tone.

Slate barks out a laugh. "Your wife may be a sub, but telling her no is like telling a Dom to kneel."

I look over to Lucio, and he shrugs, just as confused by the conversation as I am.

James finally cracks a smile. "Touché."

"Go on up. No one will bother you or the ladies." Slate's lips turn up into a sly smirk. "Enjoy yourselves."

CHAPTER FOUR

TILLY

"Holy fuckballs." Bianca steps forward, pressing her palms flat against the glass, and stares down at the scene below us. "This is better than I could've ever imagined."

"You've imagined this?" I wave my hand toward the people having sex one floor down.

Not just having any kind of sex; they're banging like rabbits out in the open.

Even in the darkened room, I can see a blush creep across Bianca's cheeks. "So many times."

My gaze goes back to the glass and the people

below. My eyes widen as a woman steps up to a large wooden X and a man starts to strap her in. She's naked. Nothing covering her body, and she's not the least bit self-conscious about her supple curves or the way the people around her are staring.

Part of me wishes I could be that bold and unashamed. Nudity isn't something I've ever been completely comfortable with, except with Angelo and Mitchell. Even when I'm in a swimsuit, it's a one-piece, trying to cover as much of my pale skin as possible.

"Watch," Izzy says as she steps next to me and points to the couple. I can't seem to tear my gaze away from what's happening either. "He's going to whip her."

I gasp, moving my hand to my mouth. "Why?"

"She wants it." I can feel Izzy's eyes on me. "Needs it."

I shake my head, and I feel my eyes widen as he straps her wrists and ankles to the wooden boards, but there's no fear on her features. "I don't understand," I whisper.

I'm trying like hell to figure out what could be pleasurable about a man, or hell, anyone, inducing pain and getting off on it.

"Just watch." Izzy touches my arm and leaves her hand there like she's protecting me. "You'll understand more after you see the exchange."

I'm mesmerized even as worry works across my shoulders, and the air around me seems to thicken. A small crowd has gathered around the couple, not hiding in the shadows like we are. A few people point off to the left as the man whispers in the woman's ear, and I follow their movement with my eyes.

My breath hitches in my throat as a naked woman kneels on a bench, presenting her ass to a man who's sporting a giant hard-on.

"Oh my word." The words slip from my lips so softly, I'm pretty sure no one, including Izzy, heard them.

"That's hot. She likes to be watched," Izzy says, and I realize our room isn't as quiet as I think and Izzy's standing closer than I thought.

"Do you like being watched?" I don't know why I ask her that question.

Sex isn't something I was brought up to speak about in public. But then again, I wasn't raised to watch other people, very naked people, having sex either.

Izzy shakes her head. "No. Not really."

I want to ask what "not really" means, but I keep my mouth shut. That wasn't a no, but it's not a yes either.

"Not with so much nudity and fucking," she says softly like she's read my mind.

"What else is there?" I ask because now my mind's spinning more than it was before.

"I could watch this all day," Suzy says as she steps to my other side and stares out through the glass. "There's something so naughty and forbidden about being in the shadows, watching the carnal display."

I turn my face, taking in her white skin and blond hair. The girl seemed so pure, so innocent when I met her a short time ago, but clearly, I was wrong.

Izzy leans forward, looking at Suzy and getting my full attention. "Let your freaky side show, girl," Izzy says.

"You know what this does to me," Suzy replies as I turn to look at her again, still in shock.

Yep. Not innocent at all.

"You'll thank me later." Izzy laughs.

Izzy motions toward the cross again, and I don't know where I want to look anymore. One scene is better than the next, each couple or group sexier than the last. "See the way he's touching her ass?" Izzy asks.

I nod slowly as my eyes rake over the couple, the woman strapped to the tilted cross and the man running his hand over the swell of her naked ass.

"He's calming her, preparing her for what's to come. Watch her face. See the way she enjoys his touch and how she'll crave the lash of his whip, too."

My heart hammers in my chest as I place my hand against the glass in front of us, trying to gain control of my breathing.

The whip is in his hands as he stands at her side, whispering against her lips, and rubbing the swell of her ass. Her eyes are hooded; that much is clear in the light they're bathing in and from the shadows where we stand. He says something to her, and she nods before her gaze drops to the floor. The man places the handle of the whip under her chin, lifting her eyes back to his. A few more words are exchanged before he leans forward, whip still under her chin, and kisses her so passionately, my knees almost give out right from under me.

"I think we got another one," Izzy says, but I stay silent instead of asking what she's talking about.

I can't seem to find words. My mind's scattered, and my thoughts are running wild, making speaking damn near impossible.

"What are you guys looking at?" Daphne asks from behind me before gasping. "Is that a St. Andrew's Cross?"

"Yep," Izzy says quickly.

"Fuck. This is so much hotter than in books," Daphne replies.

For a moment, I wonder what alternate universe

I'm in or how I feel like a nerdy high school virgin who's the most clueless one of her friends about anything sex-related. Innocent Suzy and my soon-to-be sisters-in-law seem to know what I'm watching, but I know nothing.

My eyes are fixed, my breathing harsh as the man backs away and stands behind the woman with the whip in his hand. The woman looks calm, too calm for what's about to happen. When he raises his hand and the whip whirls through the air and the tip touches her ass, she barely moves. He makes the motion again, this time a little more of the whip cascading across her ass, and she tips her head back, eyes closed and a look on her face so serene, it totally throws me off-kilter.

I want to close my eyes or cover my face, knowing I shouldn't watch this couple and their intimate moment, no matter how out of the normal realm of sex it may be. But I can't do it. I can't stop looking, wondering what'll happen next, and slightly turned on too.

His hand moves faster, the whip lashing against her ass in rapid succession until red streaks across her pale skin. I reach back, rubbing my ass, knowing the pain from childhood and hating the memory.

"It's not like that," Izzy says, again like she's reading my mind. "She likes the pain. It heightens her pleasure."

"What pleasure?" I whisper, not trusting my voice enough to speak any louder.

Just as I say the words, the man steps forward and reaches between the woman's legs. I widen my eyes again, and my breathing hitches. The woman's mouth falls open as his hand moves forward and his fingers disappear inside of her. She's pushing her ass backward, giving her body to him to use.

"That's pleasure," Izzy says with a hint of laughter.

He curls the whip in his fist, using one finger to trace the red lashes running down her ass as he thrusts his other fingers into her. His touch isn't gentle. His arm flexes with each push of his fingers, sliding them deeper.

Izzy leans over, invading my personal space, but I'm too caught up in the couple to notice. "Breathe," she tells me.

I hadn't realized I'd been holding my breath. I'd been so consumed with the couple and the need on the woman's face to pay attention to myself. I gasp, sucking air like I'd just come from underwater after holding my breath for longer than necessary.

The man steps away, his fingers glistening with her arousal in the overhead light. The woman straightens her head like she's been brought back to reality, forced out of whatever pleasurable world she was in moments ago.

He raises his arm and the whip comes down harder, and I swear I hear the impact of the leather against her ass. I jolt a little, scared and strangely aroused.

"Bianca, you have a scene like this in one of your books, yeah?" Daphne asks, but her voice seems too quiet and distant when she speaks.

"Something like this," Bianca replies, and I turn my head, looking at her.

I shouldn't be surprised by her revelation. She is Bianca May, worldwide bestselling author of spicy romance.

Bianca's eyes are fixed on the couple too, but there's no shock or surprise on her face like there is on mine. "My heroines are pleading for it, though. They're a little saucier, talking back and begging to be whipped."

I turn back around without saying another word, thinking it's time for me to pick up my first Bianca May novel because there's more to her than meets the eye. There had to be, though. Vinnie is a wild one, and not just any woman could capture his heart and tame the man the way she has.

"This is way better than strippers," Delilah says, and I realize we're all pressed against the glass, staring.

"Dude, look at that guy's cock," Daphne says, but I

don't know which guy or cock because there are so many freaking naked people in front of us, I don't know where to look first.

"Oh," Max coos somewhere to my right. "That's quite a piercing."

"I bet that feels amazing," Suzy says.

I feel like I'm stuck somewhere in the naughtiest *Twilight Zone* episode, where all my relatives are freaks, and I suddenly realize I am too.

There's a dull ache between my legs and a feeling of emptiness. A small part of me wishes Angelo were here to quench the need and fill me like only he can. But then there's the other part, the part that wonders what he'd think about all this and the fact that I can't stop staring at the people, their nudity, and the carnal acts taking place only a few dozen feet away.

The door opens behind us, the room momentarily filling with light from the hallway. "We'll take another round," Izzy says without looking backward.

No one moves. We all seem to be in a trance as the man's hand and whip come down repeatedly against the woman's ass until she's practically hanging from the cross, only held up by the leather restraints on her extremities.

The light dances through our room, shadows moving across the floor and covering our bodies. "Well,

well, well, what do we have here?" a man says, and Izzy gasps, turning so fast, she almost knocks me over.

My already frozen body stiffens further, and I know in an instant who's behind us.

Shit.

CHAPTER FIVE

ANGELO

I'VE NEVER SEEN THAT LOOK IN IZZY'S EYES before. Part fear, somewhat aroused. The same look is on the face of every woman in the room.

James walks into the room first, striding toward his wife with his shoulders pushed back and a smirk moving across his lips. "You couldn't stay away, could you, sweetheart?"

My eyes search the darkened room, seeking out my bride-to-be. Tilly's standing by the window, one hand on the glass with her head tilted down, staring at the floor. Her shoulders are bunched up near her ears like she's trying to recoil inside herself or ashamed to be caught.

Is that what we did? Caught them doing something they shouldn't?

I take a few steps, closing the space between us until my front is pressed to her back. "Baby," I whisper in her ear, brushing my lips against her hair. "Are you okay?"

Tilly's no prude and neither am I, but this...the public area below us with naked bodies and sex on full display is more than either of us has experienced or is used to seeing.

To my surprise, Tilly melts into me, her head falling back. "Yes," she whispers so softly, I almost don't hear the words.

But the thing I do hear is lust. The low huskiness in her voice that only comes in the moments when she's in my arms, begging for my touch without actually saying the words.

One of my hands moves to her lush hips, holding her tightly as my lips find the delicate skin of her ear. "Did you miss me?" I ask, fishing and suddenly feeling surprisingly needy.

"So much." She turns her face enough to give me her warm, soft mouth.

I take her lips with mine, sliding one hand up her arm until I cradle her small face in my palm. Her soft tongue slides across my bottom lip, and a low moan builds in the back of my throat before escaping.

My girl is turned on. She's downright needy with the way she's kissing me, hard and forceful like we've been apart for weeks instead of hours.

Deepening the kiss, I slide my tongue between her lips and claim her mouth with my own. My hand on her hip moves forward, resting on her lower stomach before I flatten my palm and spread out my fingers so they're touching the top of her panties.

She rocks her ass into me, rubbing her soft cheeks against my already growing cock.

Fuck.

This was supposed to be her night to unwind, let go, and have some girl time, but with the way she is now... I'm not letting her out of my sight until she's sated.

"Um, would you two like a private room?" Daphne asks, and I stiffen because I'd forgotten we weren't alone.

Tilly seems to be in a trance. Not even my sister's words pull her away from my mouth, not giving me a chance to answer. My hands are full, busy on Tilly's body and so close to her pussy, they're itching to be inside.

"I guess that answers that," someone says, but I

don't know who, and I don't care enough to stop to find out either.

"Let's leave them and have a drink downstairs. They can have the room," James says.

I'd stop and thank him, but my hands and mouth are too busy on my girl to bother. Tilly's kiss deepens, pulling me further away from the people around us and into her.

"The room is completely private. Enjoy yourselves," James whispers in my ear before the door opens and silence fills the room.

Tilly's lips haven't left mine. Her ass is still pressed against my cock, slowly moving from side to side, driving me wild with need. My fingers inch lower, sliding under the hem of her skirt and slipping underneath.

Her legs tremble as I rake my fingertips up the inside of her thigh. When I find the edge of her panties, tracing the lacy edges whisper-softly, she moans my name and spreads her legs. My girl is beyond turned on; she's practically panting with need and begging for my touch.

Her teeth nip at my bottom lip, and my dick leaps from the sweet sting of her bite. I slide my fingers inside her panties, across her slick skin, and she shudders. She's so needy. More turned on than I've ever seen her and I know it's not only me that made her this way, but watching other people fucking.

I don't give two flying fucks what has her shaking with need, moaning my name, and pushing her pussy against my fingers, asking to be filled. All I care about is that I'm here with my girl, ready to take her and please her any way possible.

She's practically dripping with need, and I easily glide my fingers across her soft skin, sliding inside her needy pussy, and filling her. Her knees buckle and she starts to fall, but I take her weight, moving my hand from her face to around her waist.

I press my palm against her clit, stroking her with each thrust of my fingers inside her. She gasps, driving her tongue deeper into my mouth with each push of my fingers, and I'm so turned on, all I want to do is rip her clothes off, bend her over something, and fuck her brains out.

I pull away, breaking our kiss. "Watch, baby," I tell her, my eyes moving from her beautiful face to the public area below.

"I can't," she whispers as my fingers still inside her pussy, and my grip on her mound tightens.

"You can. I want you to watch them as I finger-fuck you and make you come."

She looks toward the glass and back to me, eyes wide and glassy. "It doesn't bother you?"

"Does it feel like it bothers me?" I push my hard-on against her soft ass, driving my point home, and tip my chin toward the public area. "Look at the pleasure in their eyes. It's like the pleasure I see in yours."

Her lips part and her gaze moves away from me and back to the scene before us. She swallows and sucks in a harsh breath as I begin to move my fingers inside her again.

"No one can see us," I tell her, wanting her not to panic as I bring her back to the world around us. "Just watch and feel everything. We're not leaving this room until you come on my fingers, baby."

She gasps as I push my fingers deeper, curling them inside her tightness, and finding her G-spot. I'm not watching the people in the room. I'm too transfixed by the woman in my arms and the look of lust and plea-sure dancing across her features.

Tilly's eyes are fixed on the couple at the cross, the girl being finger-fucked from behind instead of the front like Tilly. The woman's ass is streaked with red, head tipped backward with her mouth hanging open as the guy drives his fingers into her at a pace I'm not sure I could ever replicate.

I slide my hand away from Tilly's waist, moving it to her breast, toying with her nipple through the thin fabric of her dress. She moans again, this time louder as she arches her back, moving her breasts into my touch.

God, I love this woman. I love everything about her. She has the ability to seem so pure and innocent, but there's an insatiable sexual beast underneath that's slowly breaking free.

Her panties are too much, a distraction I don't need in this moment when she's so close to coming. As soon as my fingers leave her body, she whimpers and writhes against me.

"Quiet, baby," I assure her as I wrap my fingers around the thin cloth before tearing them away from her skin, leaving no barriers between us.

Her mouth opens to say something, but whatever's on her tongue disappears as soon as my hand is between her legs again.

She comes quickly, head on my shoulder, rocking her hips into my palm as her body shakes and her pussy convulses around my fingers. She's beautiful like this, with her cheeks pink, her stare unfocused, and her body humming with pleasure. I plan to spend my life giving this to her, making it my sole purpose to bring her happiness in every form and way possible.

She moves slowly, turning in my arms with hooded eyes and dilated pupils. "I love you," she whispers against my mouth before sealing her lips to mine.

But her lips fall away as she slides down my body, kneeling in front of me. She works quickly, unfastening my jeans before palming my hard cock between her warm, thin fingers. "I need to taste you."

I tangle my fingers in her hair as she pulls my cock from my pants, not bothering to pull them down. She's like a hungry animal as she closes her lips around the tip, moaning as she sucks me deeper.

I can't stop myself. I rock my hips forward, following the silky warmth of her mouth. My eyes aren't focused on the people outside the glass, but on my girl sucking me deep and stroking me with such skill, I know I can't last.

Within minutes, the familiar tingle claws at my spine and my muscles lock before she sucks down everything I have to give. My head's spinning as I gasp for air, trying to regain what little composure I had before she knelt before me.

I move my hand to her chin, forcing her eyes upward to meet mine. "I love you, sweetheart," I say softly, but I leave no doubt my words are true.

She smiles up at me with so much joy, I can barely remember there was ever sadness in those same eyes. "You're not mad?" she asks, gaze dropping again.

I trace the line of her jaw with my thumb, sweeping close to her pouty bottom lip. "How can I ever be mad at you? Why would I be mad at you?"

"For that." She motions toward the glass with her head, but her eyes are on me.

I shake my head, smirking at my girl. "Never. I'm just glad I was here." Jesus, am I fucking happy we came when we did, no pun intended.

"It's so..." Her voice trails off for a moment, but I don't stop smiling, wanting her to feel comfortable to share anything and everything with me. "...naughty."

I slip my hands under her arms, cradling her sides as I pull her up so we're face-to-face. "There's nothing naughty about sex, even watching other people have sex, baby."

"Have you?"

"What? Watched people before?" I finish her question because the words seem to get trapped somewhere in the back of her throat.

She nods, and I shake my head.

"I haven't before now, but I may have to change that if it turns you on."

"Were you turned on?" She pokes her tongue out and sweeps it across her bottom lip, driving me wild.

"Didn't you feel how turned on I was?" I raise an eyebrow.

She laughs. "It is hot."

I stare into her eyes, losing myself in their green depths. "Watching you watch them and seeing how turned on you were is enough to drive any man crazy."

She looks around the room as I stroke the underside of her ass cheek, loving the softness against my rough skin. "Where did everyone go?"

I shrug and lean forward, pressing my lips to her neck. "Don't much fucking care," I murmur against her skin and press my erection into her stomach. "I'm not done with you yet, sweetheart."

Her breath hitches, and I know my girl isn't done with me yet either.

CHAPTER SIX

TILLY

"Look who decided to join us," Izzy says, twisting a red straw between her fingers and wearing a smug grin. "Thought you two would never come up for air."

My cheeks heat, and I realize everyone around the table knows exactly what we were doing.

The embarrassment only lasts a moment until Angelo squeezes my fingers. "Shut it, cousin," he tells her, but she throws him a wink.

"I think we have another Suzy Sunshine on our hands."

I snort. "I'm far from innocent, and so is she." My

gaze moves to Suzy, who's draped across her fine-ass husband, looking just as frisky as I felt before Angelo showed up.

"Are we enjoying ourselves?" Slate, the owner of the club, asks as he steps closer to the table.

Angelo's arm snakes around my waist like he's claiming ownership and needs to mark his territory. "It's an interesting place."

We're in the public bar area, and a majority of the people sipping their fancy drinks probably have no idea what's going on on the other side of the wall. I've passed by this building at least a dozen times since I moved to Chicago, and never in my wildest dreams would I have imagined what was going on inside.

Slate moves closer to me, and Angelo's arm tightens. "You're welcome here anytime. If you'd like to experience the club in a more personal way—" his gaze dips to me and then to Angelo "—I'd be more than happy to make your fantasies a reality."

Oh shit. This can't be good.

Angelo shifts, moving me to his other side and putting distance between Slate and me. "*My woman* enjoyed herself, but I'm not sure we'll be coming back."

My skin tingles at the way he says my woman. It's a little barbaric but hella sexy, especially with how hard he's holding me against his body.

"Slate," the man sitting next to Izzy says. There's a

warning in his voice, and the glare he's giving Slate is so icy cold.

Slate throws up his hands, but there's a smile on his lips. "I mean no harm, James. You know damn well she isn't my type either. Well, I have a club to run. Drink up. Everything's on the house. By the way—" he turns his attention to Vinnie "—it's nice to see you back again."

That statement earns Vinnie a quizzical look from Bianca. She stares at her man's profile with her mouth hanging open and her eyebrows furrowing, moving like she has so many questions she wants to ask, but she stays quiet.

"Thanks, man. It's nice to be home again," Vinnie tells Slate before he disappears through the velvet curtain and back to the front of house.

Angelo pulls me into his lap as he sits. "I don't like that man."

James laughs and swipes his hand across his face. "He likes dick, so he's more interested in you," he says to Angelo, "and not Tilly."

Roger quietly excuses himself and heads toward the same door Slate just walked through. Everyone's so busy talking, they don't even notice his sudden disappearance, but I do. Does he know Slate, or is he interested in the man?

"Now what?" a man asks as he kicks back, sliding

his arm around Angel's chair. I assume the tall, sexy drink of water is Thomas, her badass private investigator husband who used to work for the DEA to bring down biker gangs.

Angel rests her head on Thomas's shoulder, staring up at him, batting her eyelashes. "I know we were supposed to party separately, but we're childless tonight. I don't want to waste this opportunity. We should all party together," Angel says, looking around the table for backup.

"Everyone feel that way?" the man with Suzy in his lap asks.

I stare at him, taking in his chiseled features, handsome face, and tattoos peeking out from underneath his shirt. I can see why Suzy Sunshine went from an innocent to a dirty girl in a hot second. The man looks like sin and sex, dripping confidence and swagger.

"Yes, Joe." Suzy bounces slightly, and his hands move to her waist, stopping her movement.

"Sugar, don't do that, or I'll have to take you in the other room and finish what you're starting." There's a small smile playing across his lips, but I bet he's not joking.

Suzy waggles her eyebrows. "Is that a promise?"

I laugh, enjoying their lightheartedness and the love that comes off them in waves. It's like that with everyone at the table. Every couple is connected in some way—holding hands or touching each other some-where. There's no distance. Only love.

"Let's go back upstairs and drink," Race says with a wicked smile. "You know...and watch some people fuck."

"My girl wants to let her freak flag fly tonight?" her guy says.

"Fuck yeah. It's hot, and how many times do I get to experience something like that?" she replies.

"I'm sure we can make this a regular occurrence," he tells her, sweeping his thumb across her wrist as he speaks. He looks at her with such adoration and love, my heart swells.

That's the way in this family. The men, just like Angelo, are completely and utterly in love. There's no doubt who they belong to or that they're taken. No one's eyes wander to the women with very little clothing wandering around the bar space, prowling for men.

"It's more private and easier to talk in that room," Max adds, tracing the lines of a tattoo on her husband's hand.

"Among other things," he replies with the most wickedly sexy smirk I've ever seen.

"Anyone against going back upstairs?" Izzy asks, and she's looking right at me because earlier, I was the only one to object to coming to this place.

"It's your night," Mia's guy says and looks at Angelo and me.

I shake my head, leaving no doubt about how I feel, and gaze over my shoulder at Angelo. He smiles, running his hands up and down my arms, causing goose bumps to scatter across my skin.

"I don't care where we are as long as we're together," Angelo says, taking the words right out of my mouth.

I'VE LOST track of the number of drinks I've consumed. My face no longer feels like it's attached to my body. Every inch of me tingles, not from the nearness of my soon-to-be-husband, but because of all the alcohol running through my veins.

I'd never thought of myself as a lightweight drinker. But tonight, I feel like it's my twenty-first birthday party with the way my body's humming, while everyone else around seems more sober.

"What are their names again?" I whisper into Angelo's ear, still trying to memorize the names of everyone here.

At this point, I'm so drunk, I know I'll never remember, but that doesn't stop me from trying between giggles.

"Joe, Anthony, Thomas, Morgan, James, and Mike." Angelo points to each guy as he says their names, but he's talking too fast for me to keep up.

"Were you all bred in some hot-guy breeding farm?" I giggle again, so unlike myself, before hiccupping.

Angelo's hand comes to my face, cradling my cheek in his palm. "Are you saying my cousins are hot?" He raises an eyebrow.

"I'm saying no one got hit with the ugly cart." I smile. "Even the women are drop-dead gorgeous."

Angelo laughs and looks around the room at his cousins. "Baby," he whispers, and my heart flutters. "There's no one more beautiful than you."

I blink a few times, trying to get the two images of Angelo to melt into one, but I fail. "How did I get so lucky?"

"Oh. My. God," Mia says. "Look at this crazy shit."

Izzy and James don't move. They're too busy smacking lips across the table from us like two teenagers free from their parents for the night.

I'm too drunk to move, and Angelo's still holding my face and all of my attention. But the rest of the room gravitates toward the windows, staring out across the public area with their hands against the glass.

"You want to look?" Angelo asks.

I shake my head. "I'm perfect where I am."

To be honest, I'm not entirely sure I could even walk over to the window without falling on my face. My legs feel like rubber, nowhere near stable enough to support my body weight and make it to the glass with any sort of grace.

A server walks in, and the light from the hallway momentarily blinds me. Everything is amplified. The light, his touch, my need. She places two more bottles of champagne in the buckets near our table. She lingers a little longer than the last girl, her eyes roaming across the room. No doubt she's taking in the hotness factor of the men filling the tiny space because that's what I would do if I were her.

"Vinnie?" she asks with her mouth practically hanging open. "Vinnie Gallo?"

Bianca turns first. Her eyes narrow as she takes in the scantily clad woman holding the tray and looking at Vinnie like he's prey. Her breasts are so large, they're practically spilling out of her corset.

Bianca steps forward, holding out her hand to the woman. "I'm his fiancée, Bianca," she says, driving that point home and basically telling the woman to back the fuck up.

The woman's eyebrows practically touch her hair-line as soon as the words are out of Bianca's mouth.

"Uh oh," I say, watching what could very well be a train wreck happening right before my eyes.

"His past had to catch up with him sometime," Angelo says with a hint of laughter in his voice.

Vinnie turns, not from hearing the exchange, but after he reached for Bianca at his side and she wasn't there. "Melinda?" Vinnie says in disbelief. "Is that you?"

Bianca's arms are folded in front of her chest, and her head's tilted. I know that look. Have seen it before when some of his rabid fans try to stake their claim on her man. She's about to throw down.

Vinnie slides his arm around Bianca's waist. Again, not hiding where his heart belongs, just like every other man in this room. "Baby, this is Melinda," he says like Bianca's suddenly going to realize who she is and be okay with her and her mighty big breasts. "We went to Sunday school together."

I don't know why, but I snort. Not a ladylike laugh either. The thought of Vinnie in Sunday school, praying to Jesus and learning the bible, has me in a complete fit.

Before Bianca came along, he had to be one of the biggest ladies' men I'd ever met. There wasn't a skirt he didn't chase, especially if it was attached to two killer legs and an even bigger rack.

Bianca doesn't seem to be buying his story because she doesn't drop a shoulder and her hard stare doesn't falter. "It's nice to meet you." The smile on Bianca's face is tight, almost painful to look at.

"I wish I had time to catch up, but I have customers waiting. It's nice to see you," Melinda says, her eyes moving between Bianca and Vinnie. "I'm so happy for all your success."

"Thanks, Mel." Vinnie smiles, watching as Melinda spins on her heel and walks back through the door, shrouding the room in darkness again.

"Thanks, Mel," Bianca repeats, mocking him. "Seriously, is there a girl in this city you haven't banged?"

Vinnie's arms tighten around her body as he places his face in the crook of her neck. "Baby, are you jealous? I mean, we can read bible verses together if it'll make you feel like it evens the score with Melinda."

"You never slept with her?" Bianca's point-blank with her question.

It's one of the reasons I adore her so much.

At her age, I was nowhere near as comfortable with myself to be so forthright. I'd dance around topics, hoping Mitchell would get the hint. Typically, he didn't, and that was entirely my fault for being too scared to ask him directly. But that isn't Bianca's style. Now, I'm that girl. Never afraid to say what I mean, but I wish I'd had the balls to do it sooner.

Vinnie peppers her skin with kisses. "Never," he

murmurs into her neck. "Didn't actually think about her that way at all."

"You think about every woman that way," Bianca shoots back, but she tilts her head to give him more access to nibble her flesh.

"I *used* to think about women that way, baby. Now I have you, and there's no one else on my mind."

My heart melts a little at his words. Damn, I love every man in this family. They know when and how to say the right thing to make any girl putty in their hands.

CHAPTER SEVEN

TILLY

"You look absolutely perfect," Daphne says as she wraps her arms around me. "I'm so happy you'll finally be my sister."

"I love you," I whisper in her ear before she pulls away. I don't speak louder, not trusting my voice at a moment like this. I'm liable to start weeping, but it wouldn't be the first time today.

"You now have three sisters," Delilah says, elbowing Daphne out of my embrace and taking her place. "We're a family now."

It's funny how life works out. In a heartbeat, I went

from it being just Roger and me to a family with so many people, my heart couldn't be any fuller.

"I don't know what I did to deserve all this," I say softly, touching the corners of my eyes before my vision has a chance to blur.

"You deserve this as much as the rest of us," Bianca tells me, pulling a tissue from her small purse and offering it to me. "Don't ruin your makeup, babe."

I take the tissue and blot away the happy tears. I feel like an idiot because I'm crying from joy and I haven't even walked down the aisle yet.

"We're going to give you a moment alone. We'll be outside when you're ready," Daphne says, shooing everyone toward the doorway before they can protest.

Butterflies fill my stomach as I step in front of the full-length mirror and blink a few times. I never thought I'd be here again, wearing a dress made of decadent lace and the smoothest silk, and getting married.

The door opens, and there's a small gasp. "You're so pretty," Tate says as she stands in the doorway at her grandmother's side.

She looks like such a little princess in her light pink lace dress, which matches mine exactly, and her crystal tiara I bought for her to wear today. This day is just as much about her and Brax as it is about Angelo and me. Their world is going to change forever, as will mine.

I turn, motioning for her. "Come here, sweetheart."

Tate and Brax have been a shining light in my life, along with Angelo. I've been trusted with their well-being, helping to raise them, and to love them. Tate has taken to me as if she were my own, and I love her as if she came from my body and of my blood.

She runs toward me and wraps her tiny arms around my body, smashing her face into my dress. "I'm so happy," she says, her voice muffled.

"Can you give us a minute?" I ask Betty, wanting to talk to Tate before the wedding.

"Sure, dear." Betty gives me a quick nod before closing the door, leaving us alone.

I take Tate's hand and guide her toward the couch. She practically jumps into my lap, not caring that we're all dressed up, ready to walk down the aisle. She swipes her long brown hair away from her face and stares up at me with her big blue eyes.

"Are you ready?" I ask her, holding her tight.

She nods. "I'm so happy," she whispers again, barely containing her excitement, but she's shaking.

"How's your daddy?"

"He looks so handsome." She smiles.

Angelo looks handsome in everything he wears. The man wears pajama pants like nobody's business, and when he's shirtless...don't even get me started.

"Is he okay?"

She nods quickly. "He's excited too."

"Are you happy?" I ask, because nothing is more important to me than this little girl's happiness.

She turns in my lap and places her hand on the exposed skin above my sweetheart neckline. "I am."

"Good." I squeeze her tighter, kissing her plump cheeks, careful not to smudge my lipstick or leave any behind.

Her fingers find my diamond pendant. "Brax and I have a question," she says, sounding so grown-up.

"Anything, baby."

She glances down for a second and shifts. "We want to know if we can call you Mom."

My vision blurs. Never in a million years did I think this kid was going to ask me that question just before I walked down the aisle. My heart races, and my chest is so full of joy and love, I'm not sure my body can take much more.

"Would you like that?" I can barely get the words out without bursting into tears.

Tate nods. "We need a mommy."

My heart breaks. Literally breaks for this little girl, sitting in my lap, begging for me to be her mother. There's nothing that would give me greater joy, but I also don't want her to forget she has a mother. Although I'll always be here, I can never replace the woman who gave birth to her.

"You have one, sweetheart." I brush her hair off her shoulder. "She may not be here with you, but she'll always be yours."

"Cole has two mommies." Cole's her best friend at school, and he does, in fact, have two mommies, but no daddy like Tate.

"Yes, he does," I tell her, but I don't say anything more. I reach out and cup her face in my hands. "I'd be the luckiest woman in the world to have you as a daughter, Tate. Nothing would make me happier."

"So that's a yes?" she asks with so much hopefulness in her eyes, I can't help but nod. Her little body vibrates with excitement. "This is the best day ever."

"It's almost time," Roger says from the doorway, looking stunning as always in his pristine and overpriced suit. "Are you ready?"

"One second," I tell him before returning my full attention to Tate. I wrap my arms around her, hugging her tightly. "I love you, Tate."

"I love you too, Mommy," she says before wiggling out of my arms and dashing to the door right past Roger.

The tears I've somehow held in start to fall, growing in intensity as the power and importance of her last words hit me.

"Oh shit. Don't cry. You're going to mess up your

makeup." Roger stalks toward me, pulling a tissue from the box sitting on the table near the doorway.

"Did you hear her?" My words come out garbled because my face is scrunched up in the worst ugly-cry expression ever. It's not pretty, and I'm glad she waited to say those words until we were alone.

Roger nods. "Kid's got timing." He laughs as he bends down and hands me the tissue.

I press the soft cotton to my face, careful not to smear my makeup, which I'm sure is already running down my face. Roger reaches into his jacket and fishes out two envelopes.

"I have two letters for you today."

I raise my eyebrows, and I know the floodgates are about to break wide open.

"One from your past and one from your future," he says as he places them in my hand. "Take your time reading them. The people will wait."

"Look at me," I say through my tears, noticing the mascara all over the tissue.

"I'll get Martin back here. He's the best drag makeup artist in Chicago. He can fix your face."

I laugh and cry at the same time, tightening my hold on the envelopes.

"Breathe, Tilly."

I inhale, trying to calm myself down, even though there's no use. Whatever's inside these envelopes will undoubtedly do nothing to make the tears stop falling.

"I'll be back in a few minutes." Roger pats my hands before walking toward the door.

I stare up at him and take another deep breath. When he leaves, I glance down at both men's hand-writing, trying to prepare myself for the emotional ass-kicking I'm about to receive.

I place Angelo's letter in my lap before carefully opening the envelope from Mitchell.

Tilly,

This isn't a goodbye. A love like ours will never have an end, existing like the greatest galaxies in the universe, but on different paths.

Today's your wedding day. Something I thought about when I made arrangements in case something unexpected happened to me. I knew you'd grieve my absence, close yourself off from the world, but I hoped Roger would help keep you going, reminding you of all the reasons life is so wonderful.

If you're reading this letter, you've found love again. I no longer have to worry about you being alone. I can finally rest, knowing you've found someone to love you like you deserve to be loved.

Just know I'm happy. Today should be filled with celebration and not sorrow. Stop mourning what you lost and look forward to all you've gained.

We're lucky to have one great love in our lifetime. I was blessed the day I found you. But you've found something rare again. Hold on to that. Cherish it. Give your all and remember the preciousness of each moment.

I'll be with you today and always. You may not see me or feel me by your side, but I'll watch over you until the day you take your last breath.

As you take the first steps down the aisle, look to the future and not the past. Let go of the hurt, bury the sadness and grief deep, and move forward to your future.

Live life well.

Be fierce.

Love strong and deeply.

And know I'll always love you.

Yours Always,

Mitchell

"I love you, Mitchell," I whisper as I fold the paper carefully. "Always."

Moments of our time together flash through my mind, playing like a sped-up movie reel. So much love. So much happiness. Then the grief of knowing I'd lost him forever.

I lift Angelo's envelope and close my eyes as I tear open the paper.

Tilly,

As you walk down the aisle today, know I'm only

looking forward to our future. Although our dark pasts have brought us together, forging a love and under-standing no other two people can fathom, our souls will be joined eternally in love and happiness.

Our pasts define us. We cannot wipe away what happened or forget about what we've lost. Mitchell and Marissa will always be a part of who we are and the guiding force that has brought us together.

Today, I take you as my wife, making you mine forever and giving myself to you completely. Not only am I giving you my soul, but my family too. Tate and Brax are completely in love with you, and I know you'll love them as if they were your own.

I will always protect you from anyone who wishes you harm, and shelter you as best I can from any pain until I take my last breath.

Thank you for coming into my life and opening your heart, showing me that love is possible again. I thought my heart died that day, but you've brought me back to life and made me whole again.

Now, come to me, my love. We have a future to live.

I love you, Tilly.

Yours,

Angelo

I'm almost hyperventilating, barely able to make out the final line with my vision filled with tears. How is a girl supposed to walk down the aisle and not look like a hot mess after two letters like that? It's impossible.

I let the tears fall, allowing the sadness of Mitchell's words to seep into my veins before embracing Angelo's wishes for what our future holds.

"Oh shit. Honey, this is a code red," Martin says as he sashays into the room, holding a makeup bag that's bigger than most carry-ons. "You need to stop, or I'll never be able to fix this." He places his hand on my chin, moving my face side to side.

"Is it that bad?" I sniffle like it's somehow going to make all my puffiness disappear.

Martin grimaces. "No. It's doable," he lies.

I close my eyes and groan. "I look awful."

Martin places the bag on the floor and kneels before me. "Look at me, sweetheart," he says softly.

I open my eyes and glance at the man sitting in front of me, who, by the way, has eyelashes every girl would envy.

"You are beautiful, and when you walk out of this room, you'll look fierce."

I want to argue. Fierce isn't exactly the look I was going for on my wedding day, but I guess it's better than a puffy hot mess, which I no doubt look like now.

"Do your magic." I muster a smile.

Ten minutes later, Martin hands me a mirror and

stares at me. "I should win an award for this master-piece," he says with the biggest smile.

I stare at myself, unable to believe the work he's just done. I barely look like I've shed a tear. "You're a genius."

"Darling, tell me something I don't already know," he says before opening the door to where Roger's waiting. "She's ready."

Roger's gaze moves across my face as his mouth drops open. "Damn, Martin. I knew you had it in you."

Martin runs his finger down Roger's tie. "You owe me, big boy."

"You know I'll pay up," Roger says with a wink before looking over Martin's shoulder at me. He clears his throat and steps to the side. "Are you ready? Every-one's waiting."

I rise to my feet, take a deep breath, and head toward my future.

CHAPTER EIGHT

ANGELO

"Breathe, brother." Lucio's hand is on my shoulder as he stares down at me, slowly shaking his head. "This isn't your first rodeo."

His words don't give me solace. I'm not nervous about getting married. Tilly's the best thing that's happened to me since Marissa passed away.

But I never thought I'd be happy again. After such immense grief, the possibility of finding even a small sliver of something special seemed completely out of reach.

"I'm fine, man." I climb to my feet and shake out my hands, letting go of whatever's chewing on my gut.

"It's time." Roger stands in the doorway of the room we've been sequestered in next to the altar.

"Did you give her the letter?" I ask.

Roger nods. "She's getting her makeup fixed right now."

"Shit." I run my fingers through my hair, knowing I should've given it to her last night.

Roger steps forward and swats my hand away from my head. "You've got to stop doing that. Now I have to fix this mess," he says as he starts to fiddle with my hair, smoothing back the pieces I've moved out of place. His gaze keeps flickering to my face between movements. "Stop stressing out. This is a happy day."

"Roger, you're one of us now," I tell him as I peer up at him. They're words that need to be said and should've been spoken long ago. "We're your family."

Roger lost a lot when his brother died. He went from having a brother to having no one. A single second changed his world, right down to how he identified himself.

"What?" He widens his eyes.

I reach out and grip his arm. "You're part of our family now, Roger. You're my brother too. My family is yours."

Lucio, Vinnie, and Leo stop moving and walk toward us.

88

"You'd..." His voice trails off while tears fill his eyes as he sweeps his gaze across us.

Lucio touches Roger's shoulder. "Family is more than blood."

"Today, you become one of us." I gaze into his water-filled eyes, and his face scrunches into a horrendous ugly cry. "You'll never be alone again."

"Jesus," Roger hisses. "Are you trying to make us all look like shit for the wedding pictures?"

I burst out laughing because it's Roger. He's so manly about some things and so not about others.

Vinnie steps forward and hands Roger a tissue. "Dry your face, princess. You have a bride to walk down the aisle."

Roger dabs the water from his face, concentrating on taking deep, long breaths. "You seriously have shit timing," he tells me as he crumples the tissue in the palm of his hand.

"Go get my girl and bring her to me." I slowly rub my hands together and take a deep breath. It feels like we've been waiting forever for this day to get here, when it's only been a year.

Roger slaps my shoulder and strides toward the door. He stops just before stepping into the hallway and turns to face us. "I love you guys," he says softly, still choked up.

"Yeah, yeah." Vinnie waves his arms toward Roger and stalks toward the doorway. "What's not to love? Now, go get Tilly. We have a wedding to celebrate."

"Are you ready to do this soon?" I ask Vinnie after he chases Roger from the room.

He fidgets with his tie, gazing toward the brown tile floor. "Never been more ready for anything in my life."

I smile, wondering when my brother is finally going to spill the secret he's been trying to keep from everyone. "You're going to be a good dad."

Vinnie's eyes come to mine. "Someday," he says like I'm a moron.

"Dude, give it up. I know you knocked up Bianca."

Lucio jerks his head back. "What?"

I tip my chin toward Vinnie, whose mouth is gaping open. "He's been hiding it for months, Lucio. I thought you knew. Didn't you notice she wasn't drinking last night?"

He shakes his head. "I had no idea."

Vinnie closes the distance between us and looks me straight in the eye. "Not a word of this to anyone."

I throw up my hands. "My lips are sealed, brother. But eventually, you're going to have to tell people. Bianca's starting to show."

Lucio rubs his forehead. "How could I have been so blind?"

"We're going to announce it closer to the wedding."

"Because?" I stare at him in confusion.

"I'm pretty sure her father's going to want to murder me. The closer we are to the wedding, the better chance I have to survive."

I laugh. "He can kill you, no matter what. I know if someone knocked up Tate, I'd strangle the very last breath from their body with my own bare hands."

Vinnie swallows. "Her dad will be fine."

I raise an eyebrow.

"I mean, he has to be. It's not like I took her virginity."

I shake my head slowly. "Don't use that as your reasoning with her father. That'll make you dead in a heartbeat."

"Well, we'll find out soon enough, won't we?"

I nod. "Never thought I'd see the day you'd settle down and become a family man."

I pray to fuck Vinnie has a daughter. He'll be beside himself with worry, knowing just what kind of men are out there in the world. He was that guy, after all. The one trying to get into all their panties and every father's worst nightmare.

"Stop talking." He puts up his hand.

"You girls done chitchatting?" Pop asks as he fiddles with his cuff links just outside the door.

Lucio brushes past my father with a low rumble,

and I follow. The closer I get to the altar, the more the knot in my gut loosens.

Ma's eyes are on me as I walk out and stand near the top step, waiting for my girl. "I love you," she mouths to me.

I throw a wink in her direction and spot the tissues already balled in her lap. The woman is a sap at weddings. Always has been, and always will be. She's tough as nails most times. No one messes with Betty Gallo, the Irish spitfire who hasn't lost her sass even at her age. But there's something about a wedding that always has her in tears.

I sweep my gaze around the church, taking in all the friends and family who have come today to watch us finally become husband and wife. The family is mostly mine, and the friends are an even mix between the two of us. Relatives have come from far and wide; even a few from Italy showed their faces to celebrate my big day...again.

I turn to my brothers, watching as they fidget because they hate being the center of attention as much as I do. Standing up here with all eyes on us, we're all out of our comfort zones.

The moment the sounds of the piano fill the church and the double doors open at the end of the aisle, everyone stands, and all eyes go to the back of the church and, thankfully, away from us.

Daphne's the first to head down the aisle. She's dressed in a deep red gown, hair pulled up, and her gaze pinned on her husband, who's standing beside Vinnie. Sometimes, I forget my sister is grown with a family of her own, and I wonder where the time went and I hate how quickly it all passed.

Bianca's not too far behind Daphne, trying to hide her baby bump behind the small bouquet of flowers she has resting low on her stomach. I turn to my brother, finding him in almost a trance as he stares at his fiancée. I've never seen him so gone over a woman, but I have to admit, the look is good on him.

Delilah holds Lulu's hand, walking her tiny body down the aisle on her wobbly, chubby legs. There's no way we could forget her during our big day, but she's too small to walk on her own. We also couldn't trust Tate to make sure the kid made it down the aisle on her two feet.

Tate and Brax are holding hands as they stand near the double doors with my father by their side, holding them back so they don't run everyone over. Tate looks adorable and sweet in her light pink floor-length gown, wanting to look like Tilly on this big day. Brax looks like a tiny man in his suit, and I pray he keeps the tie on long enough to make it through pictures. All bets are off afterward. He's already announced he hates the way the stiff material feels against his skin.

Tate, in true Tate fashion, practically pulls Brax down the aisle before releasing her hold on him and digging her tiny hands into the basket of flower petals.

Tate loves being the center of attention.

She's eating up the way the people in the pews are staring at her and full of smiles. My kid doesn't have an ounce of shyness in her, and I know there's going to be hell to pay when she's older.

Brax watches his sister as she throws the flowers high in the air with such a flourish, the wedding guests laugh.

My heart aches in my chest as I watch my two babies head toward me. They're so grown-up for still being so small. Living through tragedy will do that to anyone, and the tiniest among us are not immune. Marissa would be so proud of the kids and, hopefully, of the job I've done as a father in her absence. There's not a day that goes by, I don't think of her. The kids keep her fresh in my mind, tiny clones of their mother in so many ways.

When Brax and Tate finally arrive at the steps to the altar, Daphne moves quickly to greet them and ensure they make it to the top in one piece.

Brax rushes toward me and grabs my hand, while his sister stomps up the stairs, making as much noise as possible with her dress shoes against the cold, hard marble. I bite back my laughter as Daphne pulls Tate to the side of the altar, even as she's still throwing flower petals like they are confetti at a parade.

My hand tightens on Brax's shoulder as Roger and Tilly step into the doorway. The very sight of Tilly dressed in white, with layers of lace and silk, has my body unable to move. All the air in my lungs vanishes as she takes her first step toward me. Her hand is nestled in the crook of Roger's arm, but her eyes are locked on mine.

Even though it's both of our second weddings, I wanted to give Tilly something grand. She and Mitchell had married at the courthouse with little fanfare or celebration.

This time, she'd have the wedding of her dreams. Big. Lavish. Over the top. Whatever she wanted, I made sure she got it.

I'd do anything for the woman walking my way, ready to become my wife. Whatever put a smile on her face, I'd do that too. She made me happy, brought the joy back into my world when all I saw was darkness.

Lucio pulls Brax from my grip as Tilly approaches the altar. I step forward, hands clasped in front of me to stop myself from snatching her out of Roger's arms too soon.

Tilly smiles at me, and the ache deep in my soul

disappears, replaced by warmth, love, and nothing but hope.

I don't know how I got so lucky to find a love this big again. I cursed God so many times during Marissa's illness, during her death, and afterward that I figured I was doomed to be alone forever. God and I hadn't been on good terms in years, but somehow, that didn't stop the big guy from putting someone so spectacular in my path again.

"Who gives this woman to this man?" the priest behind me asks.

Roger's gaze flickers to mine for a moment. "I do." Roger turns to Tilly and smiles.

She turns to face him, and he leans in to kiss her cheek. They embrace for a moment, and a whisper is shared before they move apart. Roger moves her hand to mine, and I take it.

This day is a big one for Roger too. Tilly has been his family for years. His only family since the day Mitchell died. We've done everything we can to include him and make him feel like he's joining my crazy tribe too. The moment isn't lost on Roger. He's just as teary-eyed as my mother as he backs away from us, officially giving Tilly to me before God and my family.

"I love you," I whisper in her ear as I help her up the steps.

She gazes up at me with the biggest smile. "I love you too."

I stare into the eyes of the woman I love, feeling the pain of the past melt away as the happiness of the future fills my heart.

CHAPTER NINE

TILLY

"Who are all these people?" I ask Angelo after a solid hour of greeting wedding guests.

The only thing I can liken it to is the clown car at the circus. They just keep coming and coming. There's no end to the line of people waiting to shake our hands, congratulate us on our big day, and stuff the box with envelopes. Just when I think we're getting to the end, the group of cousins from last night arrives.

Angelo laughs as he pulls me close and kisses the top of my head. "I told you I had a big family."

"Big is an understatement, sweetheart."

An extremely handsome older man comes to a stop

in front of Angelo. "Son, you look happy. It's nice to see the smile on your face."

Angelo grabs the man in a tight embrace. "Uncle Sal, it's so good to see you."

I've heard stories about Uncle Sal, Santino's brother from Florida, and their wild days when they were younger. Sal looks so much like Santino, only with less gray sprinkled into his black hair.

Sal turns his gaze toward me, and his smile widens. "Ah, Tilly, my dear." He reaches for my hand and brings it to his lips. "More beautiful than I ever could've imagined."

My face heats at the way this man looks at me, the devilish gleam in his eyes as he kisses the tender skin on the back of my hand. I can picture Sal and Santino breaking hearts all over the streets of Chicago back in the day.

"It's a pleasure to meet you," I say, unable to hide my smile as he moves away.

"The pleasure is ours," he says as he pulls a woman forward. "This is my wife, your aunt Maria."

The woman is stunning. A complete knockout in her long black silk gown, which hugs every curve just perfectly.

"Well, aren't you a looker," she says, and before I can reply, she grabs me, practically squeezing the air from my lungs. "You hold on to this one. Don't let him boss you around either. We'll talk. You have to handle a Gallo man."

I laugh softly as she pulls away, winking at me. There's so much truth in her words. Every man in this family likes to assert his dominance. They're not unlike Southern gentlemen with their natural-born instinct to be the master of the universe, including the boss of their women.

Angelo's different. He's bossy, for sure, but I've learned how to get my way and have him see the light. It doesn't hurt that a little girl has him practically wrapped around her finger, too.

"We're not bossy, Auntie Mar," Angelo tells her.

She places her hand on his cheek, staring up at him with such love. "You're all bossy, dear. It's genetic and sometimes you can't help yourself, but it's our job as your women to help you adapt."

Angelo laughs as Uncle Sal rolls his eyes and mumbles under his breath about showing her who's boss later.

Everyone from last night is behind Sal and Maria, plus some new faces. They're busy talking, paying no attention to our conversation.

"I heard you had a nice time last night," Maria says as she steps off to the side, making room for them to greet us.

I guess no one told her what happened last night.

How we ended up at a sex club, drinking way too much, and spending time together. I don't say a word, deciding it's best for the parents not to know the details of our evening.

My eyes move from one to another, seeing them in the light and dressed to the nines. The men are huge with that dark, mysterious edge to them. Wide shoulders, little peeks of tattoos showing on their exposed skin, and hot as sin. The women are beautiful, and each one is so different, it's clear the brothers do not have the same taste in women.

Joe steps in front of the pack. "Suzy and I are so happy for you two," he says in a deep voice. I'm sure he makes most women go weak at the knees, and I'm not immune to his sexy purr.

"Welcome to the family," Suzy says and isn't shy about hugging me either. "It's always wonderful to have more cousins."

I think about her words as she embraces me. I've never really had a family. Mine was small, and when my parents passed, Roger and Mitchell were all I had left. Now, standing in front of all these people, I realize my world has just exploded like in the big bang, but instead of stars, my universe is filled with relatives.

Her husband pulls her back to his side, a move Angelo's made with me more times than I can count. "These are our children." He motions for them to step forward, and they do. "This is Gigi, Luna, and Rosie." He points to each girl as he says her name.

Gigi isn't a child. She's almost fully grown and probably going to give her father a run for his sanity. Actually, they're probably all going to give their father trouble as they grow. They're a perfect mix of their father and mother, stunningly beautiful.

Luna and Rosie each give me a small smile, but Gigi's busy typing on her phone until her father clears his throat. She finally looks up when he moves behind her, and his shadow falls over her.

"I'm sorry about that," Gigi says, ignoring her father and talking directly to me. "Men are so needy." She rolls her eyes, and I immediately like this kid. "My boyfriend doesn't like me being so far away."

I move my gaze to her father as she's speaking. He's staring at the ceiling with his jaw set tight and his hands fisted at his sides. Yep, she's definitely going to give him more than a few gray hairs.

"It's fine, dear." I smile. "They don't get any better the older they get either, but there's a fine line between caring and suffocation."

Joe grunts as Gigi rolls her eyes again. She clearly doesn't like my message. It takes years to know the difference. With age comes wisdom and a ton of hard lessons.

"They grow so fast," Suzy says as she grabs on to her husband's thick bicep. "Right, honey?"

Joe glances down at his wife, and the annoyance at his daughter virtually melts away. "Too fast, sugar," he says softly.

"Give me the phone, Giovanna," Maria, her grandmother, says and holds out her hand. "He can talk to you later. Tell him goodbye and hand it over. This is family time."

Gigi doesn't sass her grandmother as she types furiously on the tiny screen while we all watch. Within seconds, the phone is in her grandmother's hand and everyone seems happy except Gigi.

My eyes move beyond Joe and Suzy to the largest cousin, who's holding his wife's hand like it's a lifeline. He makes everyone in the room seem ridiculously small, as if they could be part of the supporting cast of the *Wizard of Oz*. "Mia and I are over the moon for you two." He smiles, and I melt a little. "This is our daughter, Lily, and our son, Stone."

I try to memorize the names and faces, but Lord help me, there's so many of them. I know I'll never get them all right. At least not today. The hangover is too strong, even after downing more pills than I care to remember.

I hug Mike and then Mia. "It's a lot to process,

sweetie. I know," Mia says like she's reading my mind. "We're like a small army."

I laugh at her words and the truthfulness in them. One by one, I'm reintroduced to every cousin from Florida along with their children. There're more than twenty of them, and my head's almost spinning as their names are rattled off so quickly, I almost want to ask for them to wear name tags.

"You're staying in the city the entire week, right?" Angelo asks Anthony.

"All week, man. We want to show the kids where we grew up. Show them our old stomping grounds."

This puts a smile on my husband's face. "I'm happy you guys are sticking around. We have a lot of catching up to do."

Thomas pulls Angel tightly against him in typical Gallo fashion as they step forward, and Mike and Mia wander toward the bar. "This is our son, Nick."

I bend down, coming eye to eye with the spitting image of his father. He has the same intensity in his eyes. "It's wonderful to meet you." That's a phrase I've repeated more than once tonight, and based on the length of the receiving line, I'm not done saying it either.

"You too," the boy says, reaching for my hand and kissing it because he's a Gallo and was raised to make every woman swoon, no matter how young or old.

"Ma'am," James says, dipping his chin but making no moves to embrace me like the rest of the family. "Congratulations and welcome to the family."

"Thank you." I move closer to Angelo and wrap my arm around his back. "You're a lot to take in."

Izzy laughs. "We travel as a pack. Add in the children, and we become a small horde." Her gaze moves to the three younger men standing near her side. "These are our children, Trace—" she points to the smallest boy for a moment "—and the twins, Carmello and Rocco."

They're clones of their father, only smaller. Handsome in their black suits with perfect posture and an air of power about them even at their young age.

Max is standing at Izzy's side with Anthony on one arm and her children in front of her. "This is Asher and Tamara, our bundles of joy."

The kids look up and wave, their beautiful faces covered in smiles.

"Well, aren't you just the cutest darn things."

They glow at my praise. All the kids, every damn one of them, is more beautiful than the next. Perfect mixes of their parents' genes and somehow more stunning.

I'm not sure the world is ready for the next generation of Gallos.

"Your dress is on point," Max says to me. "It's absolute perfection on your body."

"Thank you."

I will never confess I tried on at least fifty dresses before finally settling on this one. I tried not to go over the top since this is my second wedding. I tried to keep things simple, but everything I put on my body looked too plain. Betty and the girls convinced me to "go big or go home."

"Let's find our tables and let the newlyweds finish greeting the guests. We have all week to catch up," Sal says as he stands off to the side with Maria on his arm.

Angelo leans over and places his mouth near my ear, "Overwhelmed?"

I turn my face, and our lips are so close, I have to stop myself from kissing him. "Just a little," I whisper.

"By the end of the week, I swear you'll have everyone memorized."

My head is swimming with names, and if someone quizzed me right now, I'd go down in flames.

"You're truly blessed," I tell him.

I never grew up surrounded by a mass of people who shared my DNA or old stories about the past. I had no connections or ties that bound me to anyone or anything else walking this planet.

"I don't know if they're a blessing or a curse."

CHAPTER TEN

ANGELO

"I wasn't sure I'd ever see this day," a voice says from behind me, and I turn to find Michelle.

She's not alone. She's holding hands with a man I've never seen, but there's a genuine smile on her face. A light I've never seen before.

"Michelle," I say, wrapping my arms around her even with the man at her side. "It's so nice to see you."

Michelle and I have been friends forever. I remember the first time I saw her, hair pulled up and twisted into rolls at the side of her head like Princess Leia. She and Daphne were trouble, wreaking havoc on the neighborhood and the boys who paid them even the smallest bit of attention.

"I'm so happy for you," she whispers in my ear as she flattens her hands on my back.

I pull away, placing my hands on her arms. "Cali seems to be agreeing with you."

There's no awkwardness between us. There could never be anything more between us, but I loved her just the same. We were never meant to be together. Her wild child ways wouldn't keep her bound to this place, to me, or my children.

"It's all Enrique's fault." She laughs as she steps back, sliding her arm around the man's back. "This is Angelo, one of my oldest and dearest friends."

Enrique holds out his hand to me and smiles. "It's nice to meet you. Michelle has told me so much about your family."

"Don't believe a word of it," I tease, shaking Enrique's hand.

I move my eyes to the right, and I see Tilly watching us. I wave her over, wanting her to meet Michelle because last time she was in town, Tilly got the wrong idea and our relationship almost fell apart.

Tilly walks over slowly. Hesitant in each step as she moves her eyes between Michelle and me. Tilly's not a jealous person, but that doesn't mean there's not a small part of her that doesn't like the idea of Michelle and me in the same room, even if we are celebrating our wedding.

Michelle reaches for Tilly, pulling her into a tight embrace. "It's so wonderful to meet you, Tilly. I've heard so many wonderful things about you from Daphne."

Tilly seems a little shocked, staring at me with wide eyes as Michelle hugs her.

"You're so beautiful," Michelle says. "I'm so happy for the two of you. I knew someone would heal that broken heart of his."

Okay. So, this is a little awkward, but nothing I can't handle. I rub the back of my neck, trying to figure out if I should pull Tilly away and rescue her from Michelle's embrace.

Before I have a chance to separate them, Michelle backs away and grabs on to Enrique's hand again. "This is Enrique..."

"Oh. My. God. Enrique Sandoval?" Tilly's eyes widen.

I stare at her in total confusion. How the fuck does Tilly know Michelle's man? Especially since he's from California.

Enrique dips his head, giving her a dashing smile. "In the flesh," he murmurs, and part of me hates him for some odd reason.

"Baby." Tilly nudges me. "You know who he is?"

I shrug. "Enrique Sandoval," I repeat, but not with the same enthusiasm she had moments ago because I have no fucking clue who he is.

"He's only the hottest telenovela star on the planet."

Enrique smirks and waves her off, but I can tell he's eating up Tilly's compliment. "I'm no one, really."

"Stop." Tilly swats his arm. "I'm obsessed with your show."

I glance at my new bride, wondering when she watches *his* show because the television's barely on at home.

"I watch while I prep in the morning," she says to me. "They're just so deliciously sinful."

Note to self—watch an episode and see what has Tilly in a tizzy, because standing here, looking at the guy in front of me, I don't see it. He's handsome but nowhere near celebrity status.

"Thanks for watching." He smiles again, his teeth looking ridiculously white against his tanned skin.

"Enrique Sandoval is at my wedding," Tilly says to herself and is almost shaking with excitement. "Where did you meet this handsome devil?"

Michelle peers up at Enrique with so much love, I'm not sure I've ever seen her so head over heels for someone.

She never looked at me the way she looks at him.

Maybe it was our past and the fact that we knew each other for so many years. We were familiar and easy in ways that didn't bring the great love I was looking for and found in Tilly.

Michelle laughs and grips Enrique's arm. "I was broken down, changing the tire on my shit-ass truck, when Enrique stopped to help."

"I couldn't leave a beautiful woman to do a man's job." He brushes the hair away from her eyes. "Especially one with such a perfect ass."

I try not to gag. The guy is full-on cheese, but I know Michelle's in love with him. I'm happy for her. Beyond happy. She deserves some joy in her life, especially after the shitty childhood she had and losing her mother not too long ago.

"So, I guess you're not coming back?" I ask, wondering if our lifelong friend has any chance of returning to Chicago.

Michelle shakes her head. "No. We're getting married this winter, and since Enrique's work is in Florida, we're going to be moving there permanently."

"I'm so happy for you," I tell her and mean every word of it.

Whatever happened between Michelle and me is in the past, and although we fooled around a little, we were never more than friends. We were never meant to be more than that anyway.

"Maybe you can come with Daphne to our wedding," Michelle says.

"Enrique Sandoval's wedding?" Tilly's eyes are so damn big at this point, and she's totally star-struck.

"The entire cast will be there too," Michelle tells her, selling her on a trip to California.

"We'll be there." Tilly nods before I have a chance to decline the informal invitation.

"Baby." I wrap my arm around my wife's waist, pulling her flush against me. "We're being called to the dance floor."

Maybe I lied. I am a little jealous, after all. I don't like the way this guy has my girl all gaga over him, even if it's more about his fictional, on-screen persona than the man himself.

"It was nice to meet you," Tilly says over her shoulder as I move her toward the dance floor.

I lean over as I pass Michelle and whisper, "It's nice to see you happy."

She smiles, waving at us. "We'll see you in California," she calls out.

"Can you believe that?"

"What?" I ask my wife, guiding her through the sea of people.

"We have a celebrity at our wedding." She glances up at me, expecting me to be overly excited.

I put on my best game face. "It's exciting," I lie. "You know what's even more exciting than that?"

She turns to face me as we come to a stop in the center of the dance floor. "What?"

I wrap my arms around her waist and hold her tightly. "You're Mrs. Angelo Gallo."

I'm such a lucky son of a bitch. Not only have I had one great love in my life, but now I have a second even deeper one. Someone who lights my fire and softens me in all the right ways, reminding me of all the good in the world.

For too long, I dwelled on the bad shit. Focused on the way I was wronged by God. Now, my life is full. The laughter has returned to my house and my heart. The darkness that seemed to follow me has been replaced by light and joy. Tilly did that.

If we both hadn't been so broken, we might have never found each other. Where would I be if she hadn't opened her cupcake shop next to the bar? Would our paths have crossed otherwise? Probably not. Life has a funny way of working itself out.

"I am." She smiles and snakes her arms around my neck, toying with the ends of my hair.

"You know the only thing that could be better than this?"

"What?"

I slide my hand around to her stomach. "To see your belly full with our baby inside."

Her eyes widen, bigger than when she met Enrique. "What?"

"I want another baby, Tilly. I want our baby."

Having a piece of Marissa with me always has been my saving grace. I love my kids more than anything in the world, and there's nothing that would give me greater joy than having a small piece of Tilly and me as a legacy when we're no longer here."

"Can we practice for a while?" she asks, brushing her lips against mine.

"We can practice all you want, baby." I chuckle softly against her mouth.

"Please welcome to the dance floor, Mr. and Mrs. Angelo Gallo," the announcer says, and the wedding guests clap loudly, followed by a few people hollering through the room.

I tighten my hold on my wife, swaying to our song and knowing life can't get much better than this.

CHAPTER SEVEN

TILLY

I'M COMPLETELY EXHAUSTED, AND THE overwhelmed feeling I had earlier is gone. The party hasn't stopped. The dance floor is still filled, and the drinks are still flowing.

Leo, Daphne, Angelo, and I are gathered around a table, having one last toast. They insisted on our joining them and taking a break, which I'm thankful for because my feet are straight up killing me.

"We know you two planned on spending your first night together as husband and wife at home with the kids," Daphne says as Leo pours four glasses of champagne. "But that's no way to start a marriage."

"That is our life," Angelo tells her as he hands me one of the champagne flutes. "We're married with kids."

Daphne rolls her eyes. "Tonight is not about the kids. Tonight is about you two and no one else. Not even my niece and nephew." Angelo opens his mouth to say something, but she holds up her hand and stops him. "Leo and I have a present for you."

"We told you no presents," Angelo says quickly.

Leo reaches into his pocket, takes out an envelope, and slides it in front of us. "We booked the two of you the Presidential Suite for the evening. No kids. Only privacy."

"No kids?" Angelo raises an eyebrow.

"They're going home with Lucio and Delilah for the night." Daphne smirks. "You two are going to use that suite, and use it wisely, without any interruptions."

"I've arranged for late checkout, so there's no need to rush out of there in the morning either." Leo slides his arm across Daphne's chair and leans back. "Everything's been taken care of, and we couldn't think of anything better to get you than time alone."

I could leap into Leo's arms and pepper his handsome face with kisses. There's no better gift anyone can give us than a little time alone. After tonight, with so many people around us, I could use a little one-on-one time with my husband.

"The car's outside waiting to take you to the hotel," Daphne says.

"Now? But what about the guests?" Angelo asks, looking around the reception, which doesn't seem to be losing any steam.

"They won't even notice. Now, a small toast to the happy couple." Daphne raises her flute. "May you both find happiness and peace, live long, love hard, and never forget the feeling you have tonight."

My vision blurs with her words. "You're too sweet, Daphne."

"I'll deny it." She laughs softly before raising her glass. "I'm so happy to have another sister and brother." She pauses and looks to her brother. "I couldn't be happier for you than I am right now."

"To finding our happily ever afters." I lift my glass and touch it to Leo's, then Daphne's, and finally my husband's.

"Now, get out of here," she says after taking a sip of the cold, crisp champagne. "Go enjoy yourselves tonight."

Within minutes, Angelo and I are out the door, in the back of the waiting car, and headed to the swanky hotel Leo owns. It's a short ride, and we spend most of the time silent, holding hands and stealing glances at each other in the muted darkness.

"I hope you're not too tired. The last thing I want

to do tonight is sleep." The door to our suite is barely closed when Angelo sweeps me into his arms and stalks toward the bedroom.

I snake my arms around my husband's neck, staring up at his handsome face. "Not tired at all," I lie because there's nothing I want more than to ravish this man with no little ears to hear things they shouldn't.

His lips are on mine in an instant. There's no time to take in the grandeur of the suite or much of anything except my husband and the need I feel for him and have felt since I saw him standing at the altar.

He places my feet back on the floor, our mouths still fused, as his hands go to work at my dress. Thankfully, I picked something sensible and not overly complicated with hundreds of little silk buttons. The soft material slides down my body, pooling near my feet within seconds.

My fingers are at his zipper as he makes quick work of his shirt and tie, dropping them to the floor near my dress.

I'm in his arms, his mouth against mine, tongue sliding between my lips as he moves us toward the bed.

"I love you," I whisper into his mouth as we fall backward onto the mattress.

He whispers my words back to me as he settles between my legs. His mouth slides from my mouth to my jaw and down my neck, and my hands find his arms and hold on tight.

"I want to take it slow, baby, but I don't think I can," he murmurs against my skin, sending goose bumps scattering everywhere.

"Don't." I lock my ankles around his ass. "Don't go slow or be gentle. Fuck me."

He gazes up my skin at me, and his eyes flash. "You know how your dirty mouth does crazy shit to me."

I tangle my fingers in his soft hair. "Less talking, more fucking." I smirk, loving when my husband has that wild look in his eyes.

He closes his lips around my nipple, causing my back to arch and a moan to slip from my lips. For once, I don't have to worry about the kids hearing, and for that, I'm thankful.

Angelo's hand moves between my legs, and his fingers are inside me seconds later, thrusting deep and hitting the right spot. "You're so perfect," he says as my body starts to tighten underneath him. "You're mine, sweetheart, totally mine."

Before my orgasm bubbles to the surface, his fingers are gone and he's climbing up my body and settling between my legs again. He stares down at me as I gasp for air, looking up at the man I love. "I'm yours," I repeat.

Our eyes are locked as his cock inches inside me so

slowly. I'm holding on to him, begging for more. More speed. More depth. More of everything. It doesn't take long for my body to tense again, each thrust pushing me closer to the orgasm my body so badly craves.

My toes curl and my fingernails bite into his skin as the wave of pleasure crashes over me. My vision blurs, and my breathing ceases, but Angelo doesn't stop, chasing his own ecstasy.

The first time is rushed and frantic, but the rest of the night is spent exploring each other's bodies slowly. I don't know how many times I came or even what time we fell asleep. The one thing I know is that it was the perfect end to our wedding day.

WHEN WE ARRIVE the next afternoon, Lucio's in the kitchen, busying himself with a dish of something I can't quite make out. "Someone looks relaxed and satisfied," he teases before Angelo closes the front door.

"It's amazing what a night without kids can do for you," Angelo tells him as he slides his hand down the swell of my ass.

My body's buzzing, still high on the orgasms and quite a lot of them in the last twelve hours. I am still exhausted, but in the best possible way.

"Next week, you're paying me back and taking the

kids off our hands. I need a night alone with my hot mama."

"Anything you want," I say without hesitation. "That's what family's for."

I love saying that. I have a giant horde of people who'll always have my back, and I'll have theirs. We've worked out a family plan where we each watch one another's kids, so the other couple can have a night alone. It's so foreign to me.

Not just the kid swapping, but kids in general. I now have kids. I didn't birth them, but I'm just as responsible for their well-being. I never even had a niece or nephew to practice with before destiny threw me into the path of Angelo and his two little cuties.

"Do you need help?" I ask Lucio when I see him struggling with what I think is spinach dip.

"Nope. I'm going to make this my bitch if it's the last thing I do."

"He got his cooking skills from Ma," Angelo tells me, which is clearly evident by the way he's mashing the shit out of all the ingredients.

I peer up at Angelo with a horrified look. Cooking is my thing, and normally, I can sit back and let someone else take the wheel, but this is too much.

"Take him outside," I tell my husband.

Oh my God. I have a husband and kids to go along with that giant family. Never in a million years did I think I'd have anyone but myself and Roger. And that man is in no hurry to settle down, claiming there are no eligible bachelors in Chicago.

Angelo gives me a quick nod before stalking toward Lucio. I follow behind, checking out Angelo's ass as he walks. It's damn fine, too. I can't seem to keep my hands off that ass either, even when it's not entirely appropriate.

The look on Angelo's face as he glances down at the clear bowl, taking in the spinach dip that now looks like green slime, is priceless. "Jesus, man. What in the hell did you do to that?"

Lucio lifts his hands in the air. "What's wrong with it?"

I take this as my cue to snatch the spatula out of his hand. "Let me finish this. It looks great. Totally delicious." I'm totally lying.

I'm pretty sure Lucio knows it too by the way he's looking at me with those beautiful narrowed eyes. "It's your big day," he argues.

I pull my hand back when he tries to take the spatula from me because there's no way we can serve this. "My big day was yesterday. Now, we're in family cookout mode. Why don't you boys go check to see if anyone needs drinks?"

"Ah, something I'm good at." Lucio gives me a

smile because I know the last thing he wants to be doing is making spinach dip.

I watch as Lucio and Angelo walk outside and are instantly swarmed by the relatives from Tampa. My cheeks start to ache from the stupid smile I can't seem to wipe off my face lately.

I'm so lost in thought and staring at my husband's ass, I don't hear the patio door open and close.

"We're here to help," Betty says.

I jump, and the bowl slips from my hands, landing on the floor and spilling out by the green slime Lucio made.

"Shit," I mutter, staring down at it as it covers the wood floor.

Betty and Maria stare down at the mess with me.

"What the hell is that?" Maria asks. "It looks like baby shit."

I glance up and burst into laughter because she isn't wrong. "Lucio made spinach dip."

Maria's eyebrows shoot up. "Clearly he gets his cooking skills from you, Betty."

My laughter dies because no one ever likes to talk bad about Betty's cooking. At least, not to her face. And if I'm being totally honest, it's awful. There are some things she's okay at making, but ninety percent of her meals are almost inedible, though whiskey helps it slide down easier.

Betty crosses her arms as she stares at her sister-in-law. "You're saying I'm a horrible cook?"

I'm not sure if I should start backing up because Betty has been known to have a temper. She's like the little firecracker that packs the most powerful punch. She's had to be strong. Raising three rowdy boys isn't for the faint of heart.

"You're a shit cook," Maria says and shakes her head. "We both know Tino isn't with you because you could make a mean sauce."

Betty smirks. "They say the way to a man's heart is through his stomach, but with Tino, it's really his dick. The man's obsessed with it."

I'm still holding the spatula, bowl near my feet, and spinach dip everywhere, and I'm feeling kind of awkward listening to my mother-in-law and her sister-in-law talking about cock and sauce.

"Lucky for you," Maria says as she grabs a wad of paper towels off the counter and hands them to Betty. "Clean this up, and I'll get busy making new dip."

They're talking like I'm not even here, which is odd and something I'm not used to. I'm always the cook, except on Sunday. That's Betty's day to make us all a "home-cooked" meal because she feels that's her job as a mother. Sometimes I wonder if it's payback for her kids' years of bullshit behavior as teenagers.

"I can do it." I have my leg in the air, about to head toward the fridge, when Maria grabs my shoulder.

"You relax. Sit down and talk a bit." Maria ticks her chin toward the stool on the other side of the island. "Let me do this, please."

Normally, I'd argue, but the one thing I've learned is that you'll almost never win an argument with a Gallo. I'm pretty sure Maria is no different, so I do what any reasonable woman would; I sit and listen.

Moments later, the other women in the family join us. The kitchen suddenly becomes crowded, and I'm no longer sitting alone watching Maria, I am surrounded by cousins.

Suzy, Joe's wife, with her effortless beauty, striking blond hair, and happy demeanor, sits on my left side, chin in her palm, watching her children through the window.

Izzy is the only Gallo sister on that side, and from the way she carries herself, I'm guessing she's the boss. She sips her whiskey and swishes the ice cubes around the glass as she watches her ma and chitchats with Mia and Max.

Gigi walked in with them but collapsed on the couch just a few feet away with headphones in her ears, so the interaction was nonexistent.

"It's nice to have everyone back together," Izzy says

between sips. "I wish you'd all move to Florida, Aunt Betty."

Betty leans on the counter next to Maria and stares across at us. "Sweetheart, look at my skin. I'm almost translucent. I could never tolerate the Florida sun. I was born to be in darkness."

"Kind of like your soul," Fran says as she walks into the kitchen.

Fran is Santino and Sal's sister. She's just as mouthy as Betty and Maria. There's no doubting that, for as strong as the men are in this family, they like their women even stronger.

Betty gives Fran the middle finger. "I've missed your sarcasm and wit. That badass biker of yours hasn't tamed that mouth."

"He loves my mouth." Fran smirks.

Not only do I feel ill, I can tell the ladies around me do too. They're squirming in their seats just as much as I am.

Izzy gags and holds up a hand because her other one is busy holding the glass of whiskey she's nursing. "Stop. It's too much. There are young ears and impressionable minds around."

I look around the room, but I see no one I'd consider impressionable besides maybe Gigi.

Izzy motions toward her sister-in-law. "Suzy can't

handle this type of talk. You know how innocent she is."

"That's so laughable," Gigi says out of the clear blue.

Izzy spins around on her stool to face her niece. "You didn't know your mother back in the day, kid. She was as innocent as they come."

"Not anymore. She's awfully bad sometimes because Dad spanks her a lot. Like a lot, a lot."

Everyone in the room turns to look at the beautiful girl stretched out on the couch like she didn't say anything. Everyone except Suzy. She's beet red with her mouth hanging open and hasn't moved an inch.

"Giovanna," Maria warns, and the look she gives her granddaughter is scary as hell.

"What?" Gigi shrugs and continues to type on her phone without making eye contact. "I'm the one who has to listen to them. It's gross. They're too old for all that nonsense."

"Too old?" Fran asks as she heads toward Gigi. "Baby girl, you have a lot to learn about life. When you love someone, it doesn't matter how old you are."

"Uh, yeah, Aunt Fran. At some point, you have to be too old for sex."

Fran touches Gigi's head, running her fingers through her long brown hair as she stands on the backside of the couch. "Oh, sweetie, I know you think you know everything, but you're so wrong, it's not even funny."

"Can we not talk about sex? It's bad enough I have to hear it at home, I don't want to listen to my aunts and grandma discuss it too."

Fran plucks Gigi's phone from her hands. "Who's Keith?"

Gigi climbs over the back and snatches the phone away from Fran. "That's private."

Fran laughs. "Until you no longer live under your parents' roof, you have no privacy."

Gigi collapses back into the couch, clutching her phone in one hand like it's her lifeline. She's a typical bratty teenager. I swear they're God's revenge on parents for all the awful things they've done in their lives.

"You're going away to college next fall, aren't you?" Fran asks.

"Yep. I can't wait to get to FSU."

Maria goes back to tossing ingredients into a bowl, Fran leans against the couch, looking like she's about to give Gigi the business, and I turn my attention back to the women at my side.

Izzy's holding Suzy's hand. "She's just a teenager. They're all assholes, babe. Don't let her shitty attitude get you down."

"She was always such a sweet thing."

"Then hormones got involved," Izzy reminds Suzy with a pat to her hand. "And boys. Lord, the boys. How's Joe handling it?"

"Well." Suzy gives Izzy a tight smile. "He's not in jail yet."

"The real shit hasn't started to hit the fan, then," Izzy says.

Suzy looks horrified. "What's that mean?"

"Cock, babe. Every boy has one, and they're looking for a place to put it."

Suzy's smile vanishes as she clutches her chest. "I can't think about that. Keith is her first real boyfriend, and I don't think they're anywhere near having sex."

Max turns to Suzy, leaning backward like she's just heard the craziest thing ever. "Boys are always ready for sex. If you don't think that's his goal, you're wrong. Get your head out of your ass and get that little girl on birth control."

"She's not even eighteen."

"And?" Max asks.

"She's just so young," Suzy says, glancing over at her daughter.

Fran's still talking Gigi's ear off, and neither one of them is paying any attention to what's being discussed.

"As a doctor, your friend, and her aunt," Mia says, rubbing her hands together and staring down the island at Suzy. "You need to talk to her about sex, make sure she understands the importance of condoms and to always use them, and get her on the pill. It's better she's protected and safe when the time comes."

"And it will come," Izzy adds.

"I guess I should have bail money ready too. Because Joe will..." Suzy clutches her face in her hands and groans. "Oh, sweet baby Jesus."

"Lord help any boy who wants to date one of our daughters. He'll have a daddy and four very angry uncles after him." Max laughs. "I know Anthony won't put up with any bullshit."

In my head, I try to think of Tate as a teenager, all raging hormones and sass. Angelo would lose his ever-loving mind. She's his little girl, and she has him wrapped around her little finger. I can't imagine what he will do the first time a boy shows up at our doorstep to take Tate out on a date.

I'm thankful we're at least a decade away from that happening. And I'm pretty sure I'm going to be the one tasked with having the birds and the bees talk with her because no girl wants to discuss sex with her father... ever.

CHAPTER TWELVE

ANGELO

"I'm proud of the man you've become." Uncle Sal grips my shoulder as we stand away from the patio and the rest of the family.

"Thanks, Uncle Sal. That's a big deal coming from you."

Unlike my father, Uncle Sal has always been a family man. He dedicated his life to raising his kids right and putting them on a path to being good human beings.

My mother did that for our family. If she hadn't been in the picture and we'd been left with my father raising us, I don't know what would've happened.

Pops was too deep into the mob and knew no other life. Most likely, we would've been pulled in too eventually and ended up in jail right alongside him.

"I don't know everything you've been through with losing Marissa and being a single parent, but to see you happy and thriving, son, it gives me no greater joy."

The three years of my life without Marissa felt like they passed in slow motion. A nonstop loop of unending sadness. The only saving grace to propel me through each day was Brax and Tate. Without them, I'm not sure I'd be standing here today. Not that I would've taken my life, but a broken heart is a real thing. Mine was beyond broken, and I'm pretty sure my body would've succumbed to the misery.

"How are you doing, Uncle?" I ask, seeing a few more deep lines near his eyes since the last time I saw him.

He and my father seem to be aging at a ridiculously slow rate. It's like they have superhuman genes that move at a snail's pace. They both have gray splashes in their hair but haven't turned fully. The lines near their eyes have grown deeper over the years, but the rest of their faces have remained wrinkle-free.

"Life couldn't be better, kid." The corner of his mouth curves up. "My kids are grown, so many grandkids I can barely keep count, and I have Maria by my side. What more can a man ask for?"

I shake my head. "Nothing."

I try to picture my life in thirty years when Brax and Tate have children of their own, but it's hard for me to imagine them any older than they are now.

My heart aches at the thought of them someday leaving me and moving on with their lives. I wonder if every parent feels that way or if I'm just more attached to my children because of the loss we've endured.

"Enjoy the time you have with them now." His eyes move to Brax and Tate as they chase each other through the backyard. "They grow up too fast."

"I can't imagine them not being around every day."

Uncle Sal snorts. "By the time the hormones kick in, you'll be counting the days until they leave for college. Trust me." He squeezes my shoulder. "I think it's the big man's plan to make the transition less painful for us. Make the teenagers as moody and difficult as possible so we're thankful when the big day comes."

"I'm not looking forward to those years," I mutter, bringing my gaze back to my two rambunctious kids.

"No one does."

Joe walks in our direction, coming to stand next to me. He tips his head, taking a long, slow slug of his beer. He's quiet. Nothing new for him. He's a man of very few words, just like me.

"What's wrong, son?" Uncle Sal asks, filling the silence.

"Fuckin' Gigi," Joe mumbles against the rim of the bottle. "She's going to be the death of me."

Uncle Sal barks out a laugh. "See?" He looks at me and then to Joe. "Teenagers."

Joe lets out a long sigh. "Worst kind of humans in the world."

The smile doesn't leave Uncle Sal's face. "That boy still being a dipshit?" He raises an eyebrow, staring at his son.

Joe's hand tightens around the bottle until his knuckles turn white. "That boy tests my patience, and if he doesn't let up, I'm going to end up in jail."

"She'll be graduating soon, heading off to college, and forget all about him," his father tells him.

"The more I hate this punk, the more she likes him," Joe grumbles before taking another sip.

"That's how it works, son. If you really want him to go away, bring him into the fold. Tell her how much you've grown to like him, and she'll dump his ass so fast." Uncle Sal laughs softly. "Always worked with Izzy."

My head spins, thinking about Tate dating. Someday, I'll have to watch my daughter walk out the door to go on her first date and know exactly what's on that boy's mind. The very thought of her being alone with a boy who wants nothing more than to get in her pants sends a chill down my spine.

"Kill 'em with kindness?" Joe asks with a tight smile.

"'Cause you can't kill them any other way," I say, letting out a pained laugh.

"Just you wait, cousin. You think shit gets easier, but the problems, along with the tantrums, amplify as they grow up."

I nod. "I can imagine."

Joe runs a hand across his forehead, staring across the yard at his daughter, who's busy on her phone. "I found a G-string in her laundry the other day."

I raise my eyebrows, and Uncle Sal's face hardens. Neither of us was expecting those words to come out of Joe's mouth.

"What did you do?" Uncle Sal asks.

"Threw that shit out," Joe growls.

Uncle Sal ticks his head toward his granddaughter. "She know?"

Joe shrugs. "Don't give two shits if she does, but she hasn't said anything yet. My kid doesn't need a G-string."

"She's going to give you a run for your money, son. Just prepare for things to get worse before they get better."

Joe mutters under his breath, lifting the beer to his lips and staring at his daughter with hard eyes.

"Thank God I have boys," Izzy says from behind us, and we all jump at the sound of her voice. "I'd rather them be the predator than the prey."

Joe turns his hard glare on his sister. "You're not helping, Izzy."

She shrugs. "Want me to talk to her?"

"We've had the sex talk." Joe tips his head back, searching the clouds for something, but he doesn't elaborate.

"I'm sure it was super informative." Her voice oozes judgment. "You want me to have the real talk with her?"

"The real talk?" I ask, busying myself with the beer in my hand as I wait for her to explain.

"Kids get general sex education in school. She probably knew everything you already told her. But I'll tell her the real shit. The stuff to watch out for. Just like that asshole boyfriend of hers. She needs to walk away from that one. He's a world-class clinger, and he creeps me the fuck out."

A smile slides across Joe's face. "You get her to dump him, and I'll owe you anything you want."

"Anything?" She raises an eyebrow.

"Anything."

"I'll make it happen." She smirks and runs her

hand along her brother's back. "Don't worry. I'll tell her how things are supposed to be, and that doesn't include fuckers like him."

"Have at it," Joe tells her, tipping his head toward Gigi. "She could use a little nudge."

"Just think of the losers I dated when I was her age." Izzy laughs. "We all had some real winners in high school." She shifts her eyes to me. "Except Angelo. He married his high school sweetheart."

My stomach knots for a second at the mention of Marissa, but the feeling fades as Tilly walks into my eyeline. "I got lucky to have two great loves."

"She'll find her way," Izzy tells Joe, still trying to soothe the anger that's simmering just underneath his cool, calm exterior. "I'll make sure of it."

After those words, Izzy walks across the yard and sits in the grass next to Gigi. They exchange a few words before they both tip their heads back and laugh.

I glance around the yard, filled with cousins and so many family members that life finally feels right again. After so much time of not knowing where I fit in or if anything would feel normal again, I finally feel whole.

Kids are everywhere, running, playing, chatting like we did when we were young. There's so much joy and happiness in this small patch of land, my heart can't help but feel content.

"Are you going to have more?" Joe asks.

I turn to face him, wondering who or what he's referring to. His eyes are on me.

"Anymore what?" I ask.

"Kids. Are you and Tilly going to have more?"

"Whatever she wants."

Joe nudges me with his shoulder. "Smart answer." He laughs.

"Just have a boy," Joe says flatly. "Trust me."

"Says the man who only has girls," I tease.

"Exactly." He lets out a low, deep groan.

"Boys. Boys," a voice calls out from the farthest table, and our attention follows.

Joe glances at me. "Is she talking to us?"

She is Aunt Fran. She's waving her hands frantically, yelling in our direction with her eyes on us. "Come over here."

Uncle Sal sighs. "She's talking to us."

We walk together, like a tiny army toward Aunt Fran, who's holding her half-empty wineglass in her hand while sitting in her husband's lap. His face is nuzzled into her neck, and she giggles like a teenager when he whispers something in her ear.

She motions toward the empty seats, squirming against her husband's hold. "Stop being antisocial and visit with me."

Joe sits first, eyeing Bear. "Seriously, man. Can't you keep your hands off her for a day?"

Bear smirks against her skin. "City, come on. You've known me forever. Have I ever been like this with anyone?"

Joe stares at him, not speaking for a moment. "It's just..."

Bear raises his eyebrow. "Gross?"

Joe laughs. "Well yeah, man. She's my aunt, and you're pawing her in front of everybody."

"I'm loving my wife. I think it's a good example for the kids to see what love looks like."

Joe's laughter dies. "I don't want any of my girls sitting like that with a boy."

Bear shakes his head and laughs. "You were their age once. What were you doing?"

Joe squeezes his eyes shut. "Change the subject."

Morgan grabs a seat next to Fran and Bear, grimacing as he stares at the way they're carrying on. "I got a lead on a guy."

"What guy?" I ask, because talking about anything is better than watching my aunt and her guy make out.

"Some asshole who's skipped bail and been running around the country for a year. I've heard whispers he's here, hiding out somewhere."

"It's a family week," Uncle Sal tells him.

"He's worth one hundred grand, Uncle."

Uncle Sal rubs the tiny lines across his forehead. "Don't you have enough money?"

I watch their exchange and kick back with my beer, loving having everyone here.

"I do, but there's nothing like hauling in a bad guy," Morgan says with a satisfying smile.

"What did he do?" Joe asks.

"Major white-collar criminal. His money and connections have kept him hidden for far too long."

"So, he's not dangerous?" Joe asks with curiosity.

Morgan shakes his head. "He hasn't been in the past, but" —he rubs his hands together slowly— "like any caged animal, he might fight back."

"Why you guys do dumb shit and chase after these criminals, I'll never understand," Fran says.

"It's a man thing, baby." Bear grips her tighter, and she melts into him. "When and where?"

"I'll call in a few favors and lock down a time. You in?" Morgan asks Bear.

"Fuck yeah. How about you two?" Bear turns his attention to Joe and me.

"Suzy would have my balls."

"I knew they weren't yours anymore," Bear teases, throwing Joe a wink and getting a glare in return.

"It's fine." Morgan waves his hand. "I'll ask some guys from the old neighborhood to help."

"Like fuck, you will," I say without thinking. "I'll help, and I'm sure my brothers will too."

"Fine," Joe groans. "We're all in, but shit better not go sideways."

Morgan smirks. "Has it ever?"

CHAPTER THIRTEEN

TILLY

"I wonder what the guys are talking about?" Suzy stares across the backyard to where the men are huddled together.

"Whatever it is, it looks intense." Izzy leans forward and squints in their direction. "Want me to find out?"

"Leave them be," Race replies. "It's probably about the bounty Morgan's after."

"Bounty?" I ask, raising my eyebrows.

Izzy sighs. "They can't take a vacation, can they? It's supposed to be about the family, and there they are." She waves her hands in their direction. "Cooking up something that'll no doubt piss us off."

"Boys will be boys," Mia says as she toys with the base of her wineglass. "They can't help but find trouble."

"Do you mean bounty as in..." My voice trails off because I thought shit like that was made up for television or movies. I didn't think people, aside from cops, actually chased down criminals and were rewarded with money.

Izzy nods. "Yep. Morgan's been doing it for years, and now he's pulled the guys from ALFA into the bounty hunter business. They sure as fuck don't need the cash. They do it for the pure enjoyment of catching the bad guy."

"It's testosterone. Makes them do dumb shit from the time they realize what their dick is really for." Mia shakes her head as she lifts her wineglass. "They don't stop doing dumb shit until they take their last breath either."

"I don't know how you deal with it," Delilah says as she picks at a small piece of cheese. "I couldn't imagine Lucio putting himself in dangerous situations every day."

Izzy laughs softly. "Doll, he works at a bar on the South Side. He's in a dangerous situation every day."

"It's not so bad here," Daphne tells Izzy. "The

neighborhood's changed a lot since you guys moved away. Ten years ago, I wouldn't have felt safe in the bar every night, but now it's neighborhood hipsters and businessmen mostly filling the place at night."

"I don't care if the bar is on the Magnificent Mile, sweetheart, it's still Chicago, and people are hungry for cash. Your business is no less dangerous than theirs." Izzy's eyes move from the men to Daphne.

Daphne shakes her head. "They're looking for trouble. There's a big difference."

"What's going on?" Max asks as she sits down next to Izzy.

Angel tips her head toward the guys who are still huddled tight and talking low. "They're cooking up something. Race says Morgan's on the hunt."

Max groans and immediately moves her fingers to her temple before she begins to rub the tips in small circles against her skin. "Can't we ever just have a vacation?"

"That's a negative," Izzy states flatly.

"I'll pull Morgan aside and tell him to drop whatever scheme he's cooking up," Race says like it's going to be easy, but I know nothing with Gallo men ever is.

Izzy bursts out laughing. "Oh, I want to watch that. Can you do it now so we can enjoy the show?"

Race's eyes narrow and her lip curls. "I can be very convincing, darling."

"I'm sure you can, babe. I'm sure you have your way with him, but with that look in his eye and the way he has the guys all in on it, there's no stopping them now."

"Oh no," Bianca announces, pushing back from the table. "Vinnie is not participating. No way. No how."

I cover my mouth, hiding my laughter. I haven't been part of this family long, but the thing I know about all the Gallo men is there's no stopping them once they put a plan in motion. That's how it's been with the three of them here in Chicago, but now with the entire tribe together, I'm pretty sure it's the same.

"You're going to tell him no?" Delilah asks with a smile pulling on her lips.

Bianca nods as she stands. "Fuck yeah, I am." Her hand moves to her stomach, and the gesture isn't lost on me. "He's not going to do anything stupid. Not now. There's too much happening for him to get himself hurt."

"Is there anything you want to tell us?" Daphne asks, clearly noticing the placement of Bianca's hand.

"He has a football contract, and we're getting married," Bianca says, forcing her shoulders back and straightening. "There's no time for dumb shit."

"Uh-huh," Daphne mutters. "Go tell him that. We'll wait."

"Fine, I will," Bianca tells us before she starts to march across the lawn toward the men.

"Anyone else catch that?" Daphne asks, pointing her long skinny index finger at Bianca's behind. "She's knocked up, right?"

"She hasn't touched alcohol, so I'd say there's a pretty good chance she's pregnant," Mia says casually. "Add in the hand over the stomach, and I'd say it's almost certain."

"It's your turn now," someone says, but I'm too busy watching Bianca to realize they're talking to me until I feel a pointy elbow in my side. "Are you listening to me?"

I turn to Delilah in confusion. "Pardon?"

"It's your turn. You and Angelo better get busy making another grandkid for Betty."

"We have Tate and Brax," I reply.

"Point?" Delilah shoots back.

"No point. We have two, and besides, I think I'm too old to have a baby."

"You're not too old, Tilly," Mia interrupts, and I slice my eyes to hers because I'm no spring chicken either.

Daphne eyes me for a moment before she speaks. "Angelo's going to want a little piece of you and him walking this earth long after you're both gone. So, you better be ready, babe. That man is going to have you barefoot and pregnant in no time flat."

"Maybe. We've barely discussed it, and I don't think we're ready."

"Keep telling yourself that," Suzy says to me. "I thought we were done having kids and then surprise!"

My hand moves to my throat, a slow burn rising inside my body. "I don't think..."

I don't get the words out because Bianca's voice stops my words and all movement and chatter at our table. She's grabbing Vinnie by the arm, pulling him away from the huddle, and cursing like I've never heard anyone curse before.

"Uh oh. Looks like trouble in paradise," Delilah says with a chuckle. "I put five bucks on Bianca."

"What in the fuck is she saying?" Izzy says, but I only shrug because I don't know a lick of Spanish. "She's really laying into him."

"I've never seen Vinnie so tongue-tied." Daphne giggles as we stare at them in shock.

Vinnie runs his hand through his hair, trying to get a word in, but every time he opens his mouth, Bianca puts her hand in front of his face.

She's talking loudly, her hand moving wildly through the air as she speaks. Vinnie's eyes widen and his body stiffens when the next string of curse words falls from her lips.

"Babe!" he yells, trying to talk above her, but she isn't having it.

"Don't babe me," she spits, fisting her hands at her sides. "You will not do whatever shit they're cooking up to do."

Vinnie's eyebrows rise. "Excuse me?"

"Oh shit," Daphne whispers. "This is getting good."

Bianca reaches between them, pressing her finger into the middle of his chest and closing the space between them. "You heard me." Her eyes narrow. "I forbid it."

He glances down at her hand but does nothing to move her finger away. "You tellin' me what to do now?"

"Damn right, I am." She jabs him with her finger again. "You're not going to go off half-cocked, doing stupid shit, and get yourself hurt. Do you hear me, Vinnie Gallo?"

"I hear you loud and clear, baby. But I'm not going off *half-cocked* and doing *stupid shit*. You need to calm yourself down before you..."

"Calm down?" Her body jerks as she glares at him. "Did you tell me to calm down?"

I cringe. No woman likes to be told to calm down. It's like the man's asking for more trouble and anger by uttering those words, but clearly, Vinnie doesn't quite understand how far he's just inserted his foot into his big mouth.

"Uh, yeah, sweetheart. You're going to get yourself all riled up, and it's not good for the..."

Her finger's back in his chest, stopping him from spilling the beans about the bundle of joy that's inside her belly. "Riled up? Please tell me you didn't just say those words to me."

His hand moves to her hip. "I'm a grown-ass man, baby. Nothing bad is going to happen. Calm those sweet tits of yours, and give me your lips."

"He did not just say that shit," Max says as we all sit there in shock, waiting for the real fireworks to start.

"Sweet tits?" Bianca asks, not giving him her lips.

"Yeah." His hungry eyes drop to her cleavage. "They're my tits, and they're sweet as fuck."

Bianca scrunches up her face. "Don't you dare try to sweet talk me after you told me to calm down."

"What's wrong with what I said?" he asks.

"You said calm down."

"Jesus fuck," he mutters and glances toward the sky. "Can we talk about this inside?"

"They're totally going to fuck," Daphne says.

"Banging like bunnies in five minutes," Delilah agrees.

"Nope. She's too pissed," I tell them.

"Baby," Izzy says, cutting her eyes to me. "She's

going to anger-bang him and use that pussy to get him to do what she wants."

"Bianca's too sweet for that," I tell Izzy. "She wouldn't use sex as a weapon."

Izzy laughs loudly. "We all use it as a weapon or withhold it as punishment. If you aren't, you're doing something wrong."

I cross my arms over my chest. "We just don't argue."

"You will, and when you do, remember..." A smile plays on her lips. "Just fuck him into submission."

I get what she's saying, but it's not how I'm built. I've never been one for confrontation. I typically sulk a while, let my anger fester, and eventually move on. Never once have I *anger-banged* anyone.

"Is that what James does to you?" Max says to Izzy with one perfectly plucked eyebrow raised.

"Oh, fuck off, Max," Izzy snarls.

"There they go," Mia says, and we all turn, watching them walk inside as Bianca once again pulls Vinnie by the arm. "I give it ten minutes."

"Five," Daphne says.

"Who's going to win?" I ask.

"They both will." Izzy smiles. "But Vinnie will not be going with the guys. That much, I know."

"Neither will Angelo," I say quickly.

"Then you better get ready to use what God gave

you to make that man do what you want," Izzy tells me. "'Cause if you don't, he's going."

I fidget with the napkin sitting near my glass, preferring not to talk about what God gave me. "I'm sure I can just explain how I feel, and he'll be fine with not going."

All eyes at the table turn to me like I've just uttered the most insane words ever spoken.

Mia places her hand on mine with a light squeeze. "Oh, honey. Gallo men need a little more coaxing than most. You'll learn."

I have no doubt I'll learn, but I also know my husband. He'll listen. That's what marriage is about, isn't it?

CHAPTER FOURTEEN

ANGELO

"Daddy. Daddy." Brax runs toward me with his arms flailing about. He sputters to a stop near my feet and gazes up at me, squinting when the sun hits his eyes. "Guess what?"

I ruffle his hair and smile at my little man. "Um." I touch my chin and twist my lips, trying to think like a little kid. His mind goes in so many different directions, I'm not sure where to even begin with this type of question. "You found candy?"

He shakes his head and continues to stare, moving from foot to foot, unable to stand still.

"You..." My voice trails off because fuck if I know. "I give up, bud. Tell me."

He twists his hands in front of himself and comes up on his tiptoes. "I want to whisper it," he says softly before uncoiling his fingers and motioning for me to give him my ear.

I lean down, coming to his level, and catch a glimpse of Tilly across the yard with my cousins. "What is it, Brax?"

His tiny fingers touch my ear as he cups his hand near my head. "I have a mommy now."

My vision blurs immediately before he's uttered the last word. My lungs seize, and my body stiffens for a brief moment. There's a dull ache in my chest for Marissa, but it's quickly replaced by a warmth for my new bride and the son who's staring up at me like he's just received the best gift in the world.

I bend down, wrapping my arm under his legs and pull him upward, against my body. "You do, buddy. Are you happy?" I ask, trying to keep my voice even.

"Are you sad, Daddy?" He reaches out, touching the corner of my eye with his fingertip. "You're crying."

I pull his hand away and kiss his cheek. "I'm happy, Brax. Very happy." I smother him with kisses until my tears are forgotten and he's a giggling mess.

He tries to wiggle free of my hold. "Daddy, stop it!" he squeals and finally manages to slip from my arms.

My mother captures Brax by the shoulders and hauls him against her legs. "Is your daddy misbehaving?" she asks him, quirking an eyebrow at me in a playful way.

"He kissed me too much," Brax tells her before sticking his tongue out at me, as if my mother was going to scold me for such a thing.

"Why don't you run along and play while I have a little chat with your daddy?"

I know she's up to something. Betty Gallo always is.

When Brax stares up at me, I give him a quick chin lift before he strolls away.

My mother crosses her arms over her chest and narrows her eyes. "What were you boys talking about before?"

"Boys?" I laugh. "Ma, we're grown."

"You'll always be my child, Angelo. Don't test my patience. I know when a scheme is being cooked up. I may be old, son, but I'm neither stupid nor blind."

Running my fingers through my hair, I glance at the ground, unable to meet her eyes. "Nothing is being cooked up, Ma."

"Lies," she mutters and shakes her head. "Look me in the eye and tell me that."

I lift my head, doing my best not to look like I'm

lying, even though the woman knows me better than anyone. "Ma, come on. It's nothing. Honestly."

She takes a step closer and lifts her chin. "I know when shit's going down. So, you better spill the beans before I find out from someone else."

I groan.

Betty's a digger. The woman will stop at nothing until she gets to the truth. She's relentless, especially when it comes to her children.

"It's really no big deal. Morgan needs our help for something."

"Something?" She cocks her head. "Explain."

"It's an assignment he's working on."

"What happened to this being a family week?"

I sigh. "This is a family outing. Instead of going to a bar or playing golf, we're going to do a little side work."

I almost believe the lie myself. I find it completely convincing, but based on the steely gaze and pursed lips on my mother's face, she isn't convinced.

"I forbid it," she says like I'm a little boy asking to go on some wild and dangerous adventure.

"Seriously, Ma? I'm grown with two kids."

"Exactly." She pokes me in the chest. "You need to be there for those babies and your new bride. The time for dangerous antics was in your past, and they're not part of your future."

I throw up my hands. "Fine, Ma. Whatever you say," I lie.

There's no way I'm letting my brothers and cousins go into this alone. My ma has no say in what I do anymore, even if she thinks she does.

"Your brothers too."

"I'll talk with them." I smile and place my hand on her shoulder. "I promise."

God, I hate lying to my mother, but sometimes, it's necessary. It won't be the first time we've gone against her wishes, and I am pretty sure it won't be the last either.

"Betty, get your ass over here, girl!" Aunt Mar yells from the table, beckoning my mother with her hand.

"You better go," I tell her, thankful to my aunt for saving my ass from having to tell more lies to my mother.

Ma eyes me cautiously. "Don't forget, Angelo. I expect you to lead by example. Your father pulled enough shit in his life, and I don't need my babies in danger now, too."

She threw that guilt right out there. She's good, but even so, I wouldn't abandon my cousins for anything in the world. Morgan's assured us there's no danger. It was pretty cut-and-dried, especially with us all together against a single man.

I stand there, watching her walk away before

finally taking a deep breath followed by a long, slow exhale. One bullet dodged. But I'm sure the women are already whispering, and Tilly's going to be chewing my ear off later about it too.

"She giving you shit?" Joe says at my side, almost scaring the living shit out of me.

"It's her sole purpose in life."

He laughs and slaps my back. "It's her job, man. If you want to bow out…"

"No. I'm going. We're all going."

"We wouldn't think less of you. You should be on your honeymoon and spending the week in bed with your bride, not putting yourself in danger for some stupid shit Morgan wants to do."

"We're family. We have each other's backs. Our honeymoon isn't for a few months anyway." I turn to look at him when he doesn't reply, but he's focused on his eldest daughter, Gigi, as she lies on a lounger on the patio. "It's hard, isn't it? Watching your baby grow up."

I try to picture Tate at that age. Full of rebellion and hormones, and no matter how hard I try, I can't seem to do it.

"It's hell on earth. The worst shit ever." He shakes his head. "This one—" he tips his head her way "—may be the death of me."

"She cause all that gray?" I smirk, which earns me an elbow in the ribs.

"Just wait until the assholes start coming around, trying to get into your little girl's pants, man. It's payback. I know it."

"I don't think it works that way."

He stares at me with an unreadable expression. "Then tell me why I have only girls?"

I shrug. "Weak swimmers?"

"Oh, fuck off. My sole purpose in life is to scare every shitbag that comes near her so much that they almost piss their pants and run away screaming."

"Is it working with the one she's talking to now?"

"No," he grumbles.

"What's the plan?"

"I have eyes and ears on everything in the city. She'll soon be in college and will find someone else besides that shitbag she can't seem to shake."

"You can't control everything, Joe."

"I'll remind you of that when Tate's old enough to date. Mark my words, you will do everything in your power to make sure she's safe from some dipshit that only cares about getting laid."

He has me there. I'd do anything. I don't even care if my ass would land in jail if it meant my daughter would be safe.

"But don't worry. You have a long while until that happens. Tate's young, which gives you tons of time to plan the ways you'll torture her boyfriends to make sure they don't use her."

"I know who I'm calling for advice."

He lifts his face toward the sky and sighs. "I hope I live long enough to help you, cousin. I have a feeling Gigi's just the tip of the iceberg."

I can't help but laugh. At least I only have one daughter to worry about, unlike Joe.

"At least most of the people in our area know me and my buddies, and they're scared shitless. But most times, boys aren't thinking with their heads."

"We never do," I say, feeling my stomach flip, thinking about what lies ahead of me.

CHAPTER FIFTEEN

TILLY

Angelo collapses into a chair near the bed, tipping his head back and closing his eyes. "Such a long day," he says softly as I climb into his lap. His hands move to my hips, his fingers digging into my skin through my dress.

I press my hands against his chest, loving the feel of his warmth and the steady beat of his heart under my palms. "Are you ready to go to bed, husband?" I love how the word slides off my tongue.

His hands find my ass and squeeze. He lifts his head, gazing at me with needy eyes. "I'm tired, but I'm hungry, wife."

A shiver runs down my spine as his fingers tighten against my skin. I lean forward, running my tongue along the stubble under his jaw. "What would satisfy you?" I murmur against his skin.

He curls his fingers, bunching the fabric of my dress, and baring my thighs. "Only you," he whispers in my ear, and goose bumps break out across my skin.

I scoot forward, rubbing my panty-covered pussy against his denim-clad cock. "You want my mouth?" I ask, staring into his greedy eyes as I run my tongue along my lip.

His gaze dips, following the trail of my tongue as he tightens his fingers, pulling my body closer. "I want that beautiful cunt."

God. I love when the man talks dirty to me. Cunt is a word that used to make my stomach turn, but damn it, when he says it that way and with the need in his voice, it makes my body throb to be filled.

I dip my head, bringing my lips close to his. "And what do I get?"

"Anything you want, sweetheart."

I smile as my lips press against his, softly at first, as my fingers find the button on his jeans. He slides his hand up my back, fisting it in my hair as he deepens the kiss. Our tongues tangle together, dancing in unison in our mouths. I'm drunk on lust and love, wanting nothing more than for my husband to fuck me.

I work my fingers feverishly at his zipper, and he lifts us both, our mouths never leaving each other. As I yank the sides of his jeans down, exposing his beautiful, hard cock, he moans against my lips and slips his hand under my dress. I gasp as his fingertip grazes my clit so lightly, my body moves forward, begging for more.

"My panties," I pant into his mouth.

Without a verbal response, he pulls the thin material to the side and lifts his hips, touching his hardness to my wetness. "Fuck me," he demands.

I do not argue. I want him. The stolen glances across the yard and watching his skin glisten in the waning sunlight filled my entire body with need.

Lowering myself onto him, I close my eyes, and take his mouth with a hunger I haven't felt before. Maybe it's the fear of whatever the men have planned that drives me as I rise and fall, spearing myself on his hard shaft over and over again until we're trembling and covered in sweat.

I lean back, staring into his eyes with him buried deep inside me. "I know what I want."

His eyes blaze. "What do you want?"

"I gave you my cunt. Now I want your promise."

Fuck. I feel so naughty and powerful in this moment. After a short conversation with Izzy, I knew how I'd get Angelo to do what I wanted. Part of me felt guilty, but right now, in this moment, the feeling has vanished.

"Anything," he grits out, trying to lift me, but I clamp my legs around his thighs to keep myself there.

"Whatever you have planned, you'll cancel."

He lifts an eyebrow as a slow smile slides across his lips. "You're using sex as a weapon now?"

"Not a weapon, baby." I smirk, rolling my hips forward until he grits his teeth. "You promised me anything, and if you want me to ride your cock some more, giving you what you crave, you'll promise me."

"Or what?" he asks as he brushes his thumb across my nipple, causing my core to spasm.

"I'll go to sleep, leaving you here with your hard cock to finish yourself."

This is all kinds of wrong. I know it is. I shouldn't be doing this, but I know I have to. I'm kind of high on the power. I'll beg for forgiveness later when whatever danger has passed, but for now, I'll do what I must to keep my husband safe and at my side.

He cups my breast in his hand, but his eyes never leave mine. "Are you scared?"

I nod slowly. "I've lost one man. I won't lose another," I say honestly.

"Sweetheart," he says softly as his hand slides up my dress, finding my neck. "I won't do anything you don't want me to do. I never want you to have the fear and sadness you felt before. I'll tell Morgan and the guys I can't go with them. Nothing is more important than you, my sweet Tilly."

I stare at him for a moment, blinking a few times as my eyes hold his. That was entirely too easy.

"Not because you'd leave me here to finish myself off, as you say, but because I want a happy wife and a long life with you."

"You promise you won't go."

"I promise," he tells me without blinking before pulling my face down to his and capturing my mouth in a deep and demanding kiss.

I move my hips, taking him deeper and harder than before. Within minutes, we're panting and moaning our ecstasy. My body is sated, and my mind is at peace.

Angelo slides his arm around me, his cock still buried deep inside me when he whispers, "Don't do that again."

"Or what?" I whisper back against his neck.

He lets out a heavy sigh. "I shouldn't let you hang out with Izzy anymore. She's a problem."

"How do you know it was her?" I ask, smiling against his skin.

"She's trouble and has been since she was a little girl. You're too sweet to think of something like that on your own, baby."

I want to argue, but he's right. I never would've

thought about or had the courage to use the thing he wanted most in that moment against him to get my way.

"I'm not the same woman you met."

"You're a Gallo now," he says as he strokes my spine with his thumb. "The women in my family are strong and cunning, but I like you soft and sweet."

"I'm still soft and sweet."

Angelo's body shakes with laughter. "You weren't."

I push myself upward to look at Angelo. "What were you guys planning?"

He shrugs. "Nothing too dangerous. He needed help tracking someone down."

"Too dangerous?"

He smiles at my questioning of his word choice. "Morgan would go in alone, but he wanted backup in case something went down."

"And by something going down, you mean..."

"In case he got hurt or the guy was able to get away. Morgan's been away from the city for a while. I was just going to help him track the guy. Nothing more, sweetheart. The other guys would've handled the rest."

"I was married to a man who thought it was his duty to save the world, Angelo. And I buried him. I won't bury you too."

He moves his hands to my face, cupping my cheeks in his palms. "It was a dumbass move not talking to you about it first. I'm sorry." He pulls my forehead to his, and I close my eyes as he continues. "You know how important my family is to me. When they ask for help, it's hard for me to say no."

He's right. Family is everything, and now I'm part of this family. He wouldn't be putting himself at risk for nameless and faceless people, but for his own blood. My own blood.

"You can help if you want." I take a deep breath, hoping like hell I don't regret those words later. "As long as you promise me you'll be careful."

He lifts my head, and our eyes meet. "I'll help him find the man, but I won't go in after him. I won't put myself in danger for you and our children."

There's a warmth in my chest from his words, especially how he refers to Brax and Tate as ours. That's the thing about this man. There hasn't been a day when I've felt like an outsider. He's embraced me completely, and so have the children. His family has been beyond amazing, loving, and everything I could have dreamed of.

I lean forward and kiss his soft, warm lips. "Okay," I whisper.

He rises to his feet as I wrap my legs around his waist. "Now that you've had your fun, woman, I think it's time for me to remind you who's really in charge."

I giggle as he tosses me onto the bed and stands

near the foot, staring down at me. "It's still me," I tease because if there's one thing I've learned around the Gallo women, it's that they rule the roost.

Angelo smiles and grabs my ankles so fast, I don't have time to react before he pulls me toward him. "I'm pretty sure I am, baby, but think whatever you want if it makes you happy."

"You make me happy," I say, letting my eyes travel up his body. "Now, get naked and fuck me again." I smirk.

He reaches back with one hand, pulling his shirt up and off before tossing it to the floor. "Your wish is my command," he says as he yanks off his jeans and kicks them somewhere to the side.

My mouth instantly goes dry at the sight of my naked husband. I don't care who's in charge at this point. All I'm thinking about is the fact that he's staring at me like I'm prey, and I like it.

CHAPTER SIXTEEN

ANGELO

"I HAVE NEWS." MORGAN SITS DOWN ON A barstool, followed by my cousins.

I grab a few glasses and place them on top of the bar, staring at the guys as they sit in a row. "What's the news?" I ask as I start to fill the glasses with beer, figuring whatever news he has will probably require a drink or ten.

Morgan doesn't waste a moment and grabs the beer as soon as I set it in front of him. He guzzles half the glass, and James is giving him the side-eye, noticing Morgan's unease. "Okay, so Quintin called me,"

Morgan says as he wipes his mouth with the back of his hand.

"Who's Quintin?" James asks, turning his attention to his beer.

"We go way back. We enlisted in boot camp together, but his life took a different path from mine after serving. I reenlisted while Quintin went on a downward spiral."

"And he's a good source, how?" Thomas asks.

"No matter what shit went down in the last ten years, I know he'll always have my back just as he did when we served together."

I lean forward, tossing a towel over my shoulder, and stare Morgan straight in the eyes. "And by downward spiral, I assume you mean he got into some legal trouble?"

He nods. "A bit, but nothing major. He has his finger on the pulse of the neighborhood where our guy is supposedly hiding out."

Joe leans forward, staring down the row of men toward Morgan. "You going to dance around the shit all day, or are you going to tell us what you've learned?"

"Quintin said he's in a house and has paid local gang members to protect him." Morgan shrugs and lifts the glass to his lips. "It just made things a little more complicated."

"A little?" I raise an eyebrow.

"We've dealt with gang members our entire lives," Morgan says, like it's really not a big fucking deal.

I tap the bar in front of him, feeling like I need to impart some Chicago wisdom to my older, but not wiser cousin. "This isn't the Chicago you grew up in, Morgan. Shit's gone crazy since you left. There's constant death and chaos on the streets."

"Then it's a no?" he asks before letting out a heavy sigh.

"It's a dumbass move. We all have more money than we can spend in a lifetime, but I'm not getting my ass shot just to grab some asshole white-collar criminal with gang members surrounding him. It's not worth it," Mike says, making all the sense in the world. "Even if we live, Mia would fucking have my balls, bruh."

"Anyone want in on this?" Morgan asks, looking from left to right but getting no response. "Fine. We'll pass."

Thomas pushes his beer mug forward and turns to Morgan. "I'll give the information to my friends in the marshals' office. Let them handle the shit. They have an arsenal behind them—and the law."

"That'll work. Then what the fuck are we going to do here for three more days?" Morgan asks like he's in the middle of fucking nowhere.

"I don't know. Eat, drink, fuck, and enjoy life a

little bit," I offer with a shitty smirk because there's more to life than trying to get yourself killed.

This is where my cousins and I differ. I like the mundane. I enjoy a night at home or dinner with my family more than I care for the chase or danger. Morgan seems to crave shit that isn't healthy, but that isn't entirely new.

Maybe it was losing Marissa that made me realize the preciousness of life. It taught me to soak in the small moments, the times others would find boring, and revel in the calm.

"The parents have the kids busy all week. We should take advantage of the time away and the little bit of extra freedom," Anthony says as he pushes his empty beer glass forward. "I, for one, plan to squeeze every bit of fun out of this week as possible."

"Well, what do you want to do tonight?"

"Fuck," Anthony hisses and pulls at his hair. "I don't know. I feel so fucking old now."

Joe elbows him in the ribs. "You are old, you dumb fuck."

"We're all old," Anthony grumbles. "What the fuck happened to us?"

"We grew up. Shit isn't all it's cracked up to be either," Thomas says. "Have kids, they said. It'll be fun, they said. Biggest lie ever."

"Dude, you have a boy. Shut the fuck up with your

bullshit," Joe says through gritted teeth. "I have daughters to worry about."

"Sucks to be you." Thomas smiles.

"Eh, I already have my bail money set aside for Lily's first date," Mike adds with a shrug of one shoulder. "I've accepted that I need to scare the piss out of the first one, and word will spread like wildfire."

"Some little shit keeps calling the house for Tamara." Anthony closes his eyes like he's in pain. "I won't even feel bad for scaring the life out of him if he shows up at my doorstep."

"It's only the beginning," Joe tells them before he takes a swig of his beer. "Shit gets worse."

"Izzy had all of us looking after her, but our girls don't have four badass brothers to deal with and protect her," Mike grumbles.

"I don't think Izzy would look at it that way," James adds. "She said you were all a pain in the ass."

"Still are." Anthony raises his glass. "But she wouldn't have us any other way."

"I think she'd have a different opinion." James laughs. "She says you guys ruined her teenage years."

Joe laughs. "That was our job, and we took that shit very seriously."

"What's so funny?" Ma asks as she walks down the steps with Tate and Brax at her side.

"Nothing, Aunt Betty," Joe says as he looks at my two kids.

Ma raises an eyebrow. "Who wants to go to the zoo with us?"

Tate screeches, and Brax jumps up and down, filled with so much excitement. Tate runs behind the bar and clings to my leg. "Daddy, do you want to come?"

I kneel down, holding my little girl close. "Baby, I have to work, but I'm sure Grandma will spoil you."

"I'm getting a cupcake from Mom first," she says, and damn it, if my eyes don't start filling with tears.

"It's a hard pass," Mike tells her, ignoring the fact that I'm crying like a pussy. "There's enough animals around here to keep me entertained."

"Just don't get yourselves in trouble, boys. I remember how you used to be when you were young," she says, giving us all a look I saw a hundred times growing up.

"Ma, we were ten. I think we have a little more sense now," I tell her.

She chuckles. "Men never have sense, and by the time they do, they're too old to put it to any use."

"She's rough," Anthony whispers against his glass.

"She's the only one who would put up with Santino's shit all these years," Joe adds, but speaking so quietly, my mother doesn't hear over Brax running in circles, squealing like a monkey.

"Well, we're off." She turns toward the staircase. "Tino, are you coming or what?"

My father's footsteps are heavy but slow on the stairs. "I'm coming, woman. Calm yourself."

There's silence in the room because everyone knows Betty Gallo doesn't put up with being talked to like that, even from my father.

Her lips are twisted as his feet touch the dark tile floor of the bar. "Baby," he says and tries to wrap his arm around her, but she moves out of his reach.

"We're off. Don't get in too much trouble today."

"Bye, Daddy," Tate calls out before running out the front door and turning toward Tilly's cupcake shop.

"I don't know how you did it, Angelo. I can't imagine raising two kids without Mia," Mike says as soon as the kids and my parents are out of the bar.

I shrug. "You don't really have a choice, but it wasn't easy. I had my head up my own ass, consumed by grief for a long time, but somehow, we made it through it."

"It didn't get lost on me that Tate called Tilly Mom. How do you feel about that?" Joe asks.

"It's bittersweet, but as long as my kids are happy, I'm happy. Tilly loves them as if they're her own."

"Going to have more?" Thomas asks.

For some reason, I feel like I'm being interrogated. No longer are they hurling insults back and forth; now they're all focused on me and volleying questions back and forth.

"Whatever Tilly wants."

I'd have half a dozen kids if it made Tilly happy. Whatever the woman wants, she'll get. Putting up with me isn't easy and becoming part of my family, one she didn't help create, is something I'll always be thankful for.

CHAPTER SEVENTEEN

TILLY

"That's it. I'm moving in here. I'm finally home." Izzy stands near the fountains in the middle of Macy's on State Street. She gazes up at the escalators and numerous floors and spins in a slow circle. "This must be what heaven's like."

Suzy snorts. "You're being overly dramatic."

Izzy points upward. "How many floors do we have at our Macy's, Suzy?"

"Two."

"This store has seven." Izzy grabs Suzy's arm. "Seven."

"You two can stand here all day gawking and arguing, but I have some serious shopping to do." Max steps onto the escalator and gives a small wave. "I'm heading to the shoe department, and I may never leave."

We follow behind Max, because everyone loves shoes, and there's no better place in downtown Chicago to feed a shoe addiction than Macy's on State.

"I don't have any room in my suitcase," Race whines as we make our way to the second floor.

"Babe," Izzy says with a hint of laughter. "Ship the shit home." Then Izzy's eyes widen as she reaches down and grips my hand while she cranes her neck upward. "Oh my God. They still have the Walnut Room?"

"Yeah," I say like I know what I'm talking about, but I don't have the slightest idea why the Walnut Room is a big deal.

"Ladies, we're doing lunch and drinks first. Seventh floor," Izzy tells the group. "If we eat now, we can shop until we drop."

I'm already exhausted, and we've barely stepped foot in the store, let alone shopped for hours. But I've learned quickly this isn't a group you say no to, especially now that they're family.

Within minutes, we're seated at a large table in the center of the Walnut Room. It's a grand space with dark wood and wrought iron.

"It's just as I remember it," Izzy says, holding her

menu but not bothering to look at it. She's too busy taking in the timeless beauty of the restaurant.

"It never changed much over the years," Bianca says, glancing around the space like Izzy. "My father always brought us here the day after Thanksgiving."

"Mine too," Izzy says quickly. "We always took the train downtown and spent all day shopping, with lunch at the Walnut Room to see the Christmas tree."

I can't imagine growing up near a store like this or near a big city. The town I grew up in had very few stores with a small city center. The shopping was dismal at best, and the restaurants didn't require more than jeans as proper attire.

My parents' idea of a day after Thanksgiving shopping spree was a few hours in Kmart, waiting for the next blue light special. We didn't have fancy department stores or swanky restaurants within a hundred miles of our small Georgia town.

"Do you miss Chicago?" I ask Izzy.

She shakes her head. "A small part of me still feels like this is home, but I could never leave the blue skies and sandy beaches for all the traffic and cement."

"Why don't you go to college here, kid?" Izzy says to Gigi when she finally puts her phone down.

Gigi's eyes widen. "It snows here, Auntie. I would wither away and die here. My body needs sunshine to live."

"You're just as overdramatic as Izzy," Max snorts.

"We get sunshine, Gigi," Daphne tells her. "It's cold as fuck in the winter, but we get some sunny days."

"Some?" Gigi gasps. "Well, that changes everything." She pauses for a moment, giving Daphne a lopsided smile. "Not."

"The boys are hot here," Delilah says like that's enough to make the girl change her mind.

Gigi shakes her head and laughs. "There're some pretty boys, but I like mine a little more on the..."

"Don't say it." Suzy covers her mouth as if the mere thought of her daughter being attracted to someone makes her ill.

"Ma, come on. Look around." Gigi motions to the people in the restaurant. "You know my type, and this isn't it."

"You like the country boys?" I ask, remembering my fascination with rugged country boys and their badass pickup trucks.

I always thought I'd marry a country boy and live on a farm, surrounded by acres of animals and forest. But that didn't seem to be part of my plan. Now I have a tiny patch of grass in one of the biggest cities in the US. Although Angelo has the manly man thing nailed, he most certainly is not a redneck.

"I don't like them so pretty, more a little rough around the edges."

"Then why are you dating that dipshit?" Angel asks, twirling a piece of her dark red hair around her finger. "'Cause you're describing your daddy, and that kid—whatever the fuck his name is—is most certainly not."

Gigi gags a little. "I don't like men like my father. That's just ew, Auntie Angel, and his name is Keith, by the way."

"He's a needy fucker, kid," Izzy tells her. "What are you going to do when you go away to college?"

Gigi pushes her brown hair off her shoulder and straightens her back. "I'm going to school in Florida, and Keith's going away to California. We know we won't be able to do the long-distance thing and that our time is limited."

"Thank fuck," Suzy whispers into her menu, pretending to be more interested in the food than what her daughter's saying.

"I plan to spend my summers at Inked, learning the shop and business side of things so I can take over someday. I won't have time for a relationship, at least nothing serious, so I put up with Keith's neediness because I know we have an end date."

"It's probably the only reason your daddy hasn't

killed the kid either," Max says. "Oh my god. They have chicken potpie."

And like that, the conversation changes.

"Ladies, what can I get you to drink?" the waiter asks as he stands at the end of the table.

Everyone orders wine, except Gigi and Bianca, which doesn't go unnoticed as there's a moment of awkward silence after the waiter walks away.

"So, how far along are you?" Mia asks, staring at Bianca from across the table.

The awkward silence is back as Bianca's mouth opens and closes, but no words come out. All eyes are on her, waiting for an answer.

"It's a secret," I say, answering for her. "They don't want anyone to know."

"No one can know," Bianca says with all the color drained from her face. "Not yet."

"Why?" Izzy asks.

"Because my parents will go crazy. We're not married yet."

Mia chuckles. "You're not going to be able to hide it much longer, so be ready to make the announcement and don't worry about the blowback."

"You're engaged for Christ's sake," Delilah says and shakes her head. "I'm sure they'll understand."

"Maybe you two should elope, then you can say you were married when it happened," I add.

Bianca gasps. "We have to get married at St. Catherine's."

Izzy shakes her head. "Elope and then renew your vows at St. Catherine's after you spill the news to your parents that you're preggers and already married."

Bianca's hand covers her stomach. "I don't know what to do."

"Well, you two better think quick because you're running out of time. I was as big as a whale when I was pregnant," Daphne says, giving the waiter a quick nod as he places a wineglass in front of her.

"Are we ready to order?" he asks.

Bianca looks relieved that the conversation is over and our attention is elsewhere. I don't envy her—not her youth or owing an explanation to her parents about getting knocked up before taking her vows.

"You two already working on my next niece or nephew?" Daphne asks.

"We've gone over this before, Daphne. If it happens, it happens." I shrug, but there's a part of me that wants to scream yes from the rooftops. "If not, that's okay too. We have Tate and Brax, and they're more than a handful."

"You're past the dreaded diaper phase. I wouldn't start over if I were you," Delilah says, placing her hand over mine. "You get the joy of having kids without the stretch marks and weak bladder. Count yourself lucky."

"Your body is tight and perky," Max says. "Enjoy the hell out of that."

I wouldn't call my body either of those words, but it's nice to hear. "Oh, please. It's not like you guys have saggy tits and stomach pouches."

"It's amazing what good underwear and a killer bra can do." Mia laughs. "Don't let the polished exterior fool you. When I get naked, everything heads for the floor."

"Jesus, I found a gray pube last week, too. I nearly died," Izzy says, and I jerk my head back at the candor of her words.

"Gross, Auntie. Don't talk about such things. That doesn't really happen, does it?" Gigi looks absolutely horrified.

Suzy's holding her face in her hands, muttering into her palm as she shakes her head, but that doesn't stop the conversation from happening.

"Gigi." Izzy straightens her back and leans over the table, dropping her voice. "As you get older, every bit of hair you have turns gray."

Gigi blanches. "Oh, dear God. What do you do?"

"Wax, tweeze, or let it happen," Izzy says casually as she picks up her wine and takes a sip.

"Girl, you can't tweeze them. Jesus. Do you know how painful that is?" Angel grimaces.

"I know firsthand, chick. Shit is awful."

"I always thought of you as a Brazilian type of woman," Max adds like we're talking about dresses and not the hair around our vaginas.

Izzy drags her hand down her face. "I used to be, but then I stopped when I got pregnant and just never went back. But it looks like I'm about to restart my standing appointment again because gray pubes are not happening."

Gigi picks up her phone, trying to hide her shocked and disgusted face. "I can't listen to this anymore. You guys are freaking me out."

"Someday, when you find your first gray hair, you'll remember this conversation, sweetie." Izzy gives her niece a smile. "Trust me, experiencing it is way more horrifying than hearing about it."

"I'm not listening," Gigi sings into her phone screen. "This is way too much information and over-sharing from all of you, not to mention gross and the things nightmares of made of."

Aging is a nightmare. No one tells you that shit when you're young. They're too busy telling you how fabulous your thirties and forties are to give you the real truth. How things move south, tits and ass included, and how your skin starts to look more like crumpled tissue paper than the supple silk it used to.

"I have an idea," Daphne says, thankfully rescuing us from the topic of aging. "Why don't you guys get married at city hall this week while the family is all here?"

Delilah claps her hands together. "That's a great idea. Come on, Bianca. We'll find you the perfect dress today, and you can be married before the weekend."

"I don't know. I'd have to talk to Vinnie about it."

"He'll say yes," Daphne tells her. "He's practically jumping out of his skin to slip that ring on your finger."

"I'll talk to him." Bianca smiles, still resting her hand on her stomach. "I'm sick of hiding the pregnancy."

"You may be hiding it from your parents, but we all kind of knew," I say.

"Your tits alone give it away." Daphne laughs.

Bianca's eyes widen as her head tips downward toward her breasts. "They're freakishly large."

"Everything is supersized when you're pregnant. Just wait. Those babies aren't done growing, and neither is your ass." Delilah smirks. "Lucio loved my pregnant body."

"Again, TMI," Gigi announces with her eyebrows drawn together and her fingers busy on her phone.

All the talk of pregnancy has my mind reeling and

a small part of my chest aching to understand what they experienced. The feeling of a baby moving inside my body. The moment you first hold your baby in your arms, knowing you created a small human.

So many things I missed out on after losing Mitchell. Years of my life gone, but not wasted. I'd met Angelo because of those years spent alone. Having a baby with Mitchell would've been hard. He was barely home, and even when he wasn't deployed, he was constantly busy with work and prepping for the next mission. I would've been essentially a single mother, and I don't know how I would've handled his death with a little one to look after. I was barely able to look after myself, let alone another person who would've depended on me for everything.

A small sliver of me is jealous of these women. They never experienced the complete anguish of losing the man they loved, but they knew the joy of having a baby. I'm not sure they really understood how very blessed they were. I wasn't cursed, but my life had never taken an easy path.

CHAPTER EIGHTEEN

ANGELO

"This is the shit, man," Mike says to Leo as he fills his plate with food. "Dad used to take us to the Cubs games when we were young, and the seats were great, but nothing like this."

The Diamond Suites are indeed the shit. I'm not sure I could ever sit in the cheap seats again after experiencing something like as over the top as this. There are flat-screen televisions, comfy chairs, air conditioning, and an unlimited supply of food and drinks. What more can a guy ask for to enjoy a baseball game?

"The parents are missing out on a great night,"

Thomas says as he stands next to Mike, eyeing the food.

"You know Dad. He has to see the Cubs, and between him and Uncle Santino, they're going to make our kids Cubs fans too."

"Or at least die trying." Thomas laughs.

The Gallo family obsession with the Cubs runs deep. They cheered the team since their childhood and even without a World Series win, they kept the faith.

"They're in a suite there too," Leo announces. "The hotel chain has suites at both stadiums for our high-class clientele and business partners."

"Holy fuck. That has to cost a fortune," I say as I walk up behind Tilly and wrap my arms around her waist, placing my hands on her stomach. "Are you okay, baby?"

She tips her head to the side, resting her forehead against my cheek. "I'm fine."

I know she's not. She's quiet, and Tilly's rarely quiet. She's usually so full of life and so talkative, sometimes my ears start to ring, but I'm not complaining. I like my woman chatty, and I love her happy more than anything.

I hold her tighter, resting my face in the crook of her neck. "Something's eating you."

She exhales. "No, I'm good."

The exhale gave it away. Something's on her mind,

but she isn't in the sharing mood. Whatever it is, I want to set it right and make my girl happy, but now isn't the place. And until she's ready to tell me what's wrong, I can't force her to speak.

"Tilly, want a glass of wine?" Daphne asks as she pulls the cork out of a bottle of white.

"I'd love one," Tilly says, giving my hands a quick pat, which is like giving me the brush-off.

I let her go but watch her closely. Tilly's face brightens as she grabs the wine and speaks quietly with my sister.

"What's wrong?" Joe asks as I stand in the middle of the room, staring at my wife.

I shrug. "I don't know. She's off today."

Joe places his arm on my shoulder. "She's probably overwhelmed, man. We're a lot to digest at once."

"Maybe you're right."

Maybe it's just the number of people who have been here this week and all the family events that are wearing her down. Maybe she's thinking of the family she missed out on since her parents passed away. There're so many variables that could be setting her off this week that I didn't even consider when my mother planned a family reunion centered around our wedding.

Joe grabs a beer from the fridge and hands it to me. "Don't let your mind wander places it shouldn't. Suzy has so many mood swings, half the time I don't know if she's pissed or happy. It's just how shit is sometimes. We'll be gone in a few days, and things will be back to normal."

"Hey, asshats, come down here and sit with us!" Anthony yells from the outside seats, facing the field. "Let the ladies be. They could use a break from you two, hovering over them."

"Your brother's annoying," I tell Joe as I take a sip of the beer.

"Man, they're all a pain in my ass." Joe smiles.

I can't disagree, but I know we both love our siblings and couldn't imagine life without them. I'm sure there's a part of Tilly that has to wonder how her life would've been different if she weren't an only child.

We're halfway down the stairs to the seats when Vinnie says, "Bianca and I have an announcement."

I stop and turn around, shocked and happy he's finally going to tell the family he and Bianca are expecting their first child.

He grabs Bianca and pulls her close, throwing his arm around her shoulders. "We've decided to get married at city hall tomorrow afternoon, and it would mean a lot to us if you'd celebrate with us. But none of the parents can know. We want it to be a total surprise for them."

"City hall?" Lucio asks, rubbing the back of his neck and gawking at my brother in confusion.

"We'll do the big church wedding later, but we don't want to wait another minute to become husband and wife." Vinnie stares down at Bianca and smiles.

I wait, expecting the other surprise to pop from his lips, but instead, he says, "Pizza and beer at Vito & Nick's afterward. Remember, don't tell the parents anything."

My brother always does stuff the hard way or, should I say, differently. I shouldn't be surprised he didn't drop the pregnancy news just yet, especially without my mother here. She'd pull his hair for doing it when she wasn't around.

"You tell us when, and we'll be there, kid," Mike says with a quick chin lift.

The girls rush to Bianca's side, hugging her and telling her how excited they are.

I pull my brother to the side. "You finally going to come clean?"

He shoves his hand into his pocket. "Tomorrow at dinner after we're married. You know Ma and Pop have to be there for me to announce it. Ma would straight up kill me."

"I'm pretty sure everyone here already knows," I tell him.

He raises his eyebrows. "How?"

I slap him on the back and laugh. "After you spend nine months with a pregnant woman, you'll be able to spot one from a mile away, little brother. It doesn't help that Bianca's suddenly stopped drinking and keeps resting her hand against her stomach like she's literally holding a secret."

His gaze drifts to Bianca, who is, in fact, holding her stomach as she chats with the girls. "Well, just one more day and it won't matter. We'll be married, and her parents can't ship her off to a convent somewhere."

"I don't think shit works like that anymore." I laugh. "But you have a better chance of her father not punching you in the face when he hears the news."

"I plan to be as far away from him as possible when we make the announcement. I won't take any chances. It's not like I can fight the man. It's her father, after all."

"Well, you never did anything the easy way," I say with a smile before pulling him into a hug. "Fatherhood will be good for you."

He doesn't look convinced. He looks like a nervous wreck, which was exactly how I felt when Tate was on the way. I thought I wasn't ready, but then again, I'm not sure anyone really is. There's no way to prepare for the sleepless nights, the endless diapers, and constant feedings. Your time is no longer your own, and the realization of the commitment you've made by creating the tiny human doesn't hit you square in the face until it's too late.

"I'm scared, man."

I pull back and grab his shoulders. "We all were. It's normal, and you have all of us to help you through the hard shit."

"Will you come to city hall tomorrow as my witness and best man?" he asks.

"There's nowhere else I'd rather be, brother. It would be my honor to be your best man."

I hug him again, being way more touchy-feely with Vinnie than I probably have ever been in my life. But he's growing up and we're getting older, and the age difference doesn't seem to be as big anymore. We're going to both be fathers, and this is a time to celebrate.

I spot Tilly across the room, staring at the table of food, and I walk toward her, needing to know what's wrong and unable to wait any longer.

I grab her hips and turn her to face me. "Baby, what's wrong? Tell me. It's killing me."

She places her hand on my chest and smiles up at me. "Nothing, sweetheart. I'm just overwhelmed. I promise there's nothing wrong. I'm just tired from this long, but very exciting week."

I press my lips to her forehead, smelling the sweetness of her skin. "I understand. Only a few more days and things will be quieter."

She wraps her arms around my middle. "I love having them here. It's been nice getting to know everyone, baby."

"Yes, but it's also nice to get back to our life," I tell her against her hair as I close my eyes. "I love the little world we've created."

"Me too," she says softly, curling her fingers into the back of my T-shirt.

"I ordered champagne," Daphne announces. "My brother's getting married!"

"You're really lucky, Angelo," Tilly says softly into my shirt. "You have all these people in your life."

I stare down at her, placing my finger under her chin and forcing her eyes to mine. "They're in your life too, Tilly. They're every bit as much your family now as they are mine."

She smiles, but there's still sadness in her eyes. "I know. I wish I'd had cousins and siblings when I was young. Someone I could've bonded with and had inside jokes with and to tell stories about when we were young. I don't have that. I never will."

"Baby," I whisper and touch my lips to her mouth as I keep my gaze fixed on hers. "We'll make new memories and inside jokes. Before too long, we'll be old and have stories of when we were young."

"Oh God. I'm not ready to get old."

"We have a lot of years before we get there, sweetheart. But you're not alone anymore. You have three sisters, four brothers, and a bunch of cousins."

Her smile brightens. "I do—and the most wonderful, loving husband in the world."

"That too," I say with a smirk. "You did get pretty lucky."

"Hey, what happened about the thing?"

"The thing?" I ask.

She nods. "The man Morgan was going after?"

"We decided not to do it. It was too dangerous, and none of us wanted to put our lives at risk. We're too old for that shit, and I have a wife and kids to take care of."

The tension that had filled her seems to evaporate as she sags against me. "Thank God. I was so worried."

"Tilly, don't hold back your feelings about anything. I always want you to be happy, and I never want you to worry that something bad will happen."

She rests her cheek against my chest, holding me tighter than before. "I can't lose you. Losing you would kill me, Angelo. Not only would I lose you, but I'd lose this family too."

"You'd never lose this family. Once you're in, you're stuck for life. They wouldn't let you go without a fight. But I'm not going anywhere anytime soon, Til. I promise not to be an idiot and to always think of you first."

I wonder if Tilly will ever let her guard down about

something happening to me. I get it, though. After losing Marissa, I worry about what may come, but I know shit's out of my hands. Only time will tell what the future holds, and no matter how hard I try, I can't control what happens next.

CHAPTER NINETEEN

TILLY

Everyone's inside, but I needed a moment alone, preferring to sit on the front porch and listen to the distant noise of the city. My ears are practically ringing from the multiple conversations happening at once inside the house.

"Mind if I come out?" Suzy asks from the front door, holding two glasses of wine. "You can totally say no."

"Come out." I pat the space next to me on the swing. "Sit, please."

She walks slowly, letting the screen door close softly behind her. Not like anyone inside would hear it.

I'm pretty sure they can't actually hear what anyone is saying with the volume at which they're all speaking and the fact that they're all doing it at once.

She hands me a glass before sitting down next to me. "Needed a break from everyone?" she asks, turning toward me and tucking her leg under her body.

"Not really. I just needed a moment to wrap my head around the ways my life has changed."

"Well." She takes a quick sip before resting the wineglass against her knee. "I remember how overwhelmed I was when I met Joe and then his entire family. No one was married yet, so the group was smaller, but still a lot to take in."

"I had Mitchell and Roger for so long, and it was just the three of us—and then the two of us. I've never been around a large family. Even when my parents were alive, we didn't have anyone but the three of us."

Suzy grabs my hand. "It was the same for me. I mean, my parents are alive, but we aren't close. And I have a sister, but she's a bitch. So even though I *had* them, I didn't have them. When I met the Gallos, it was shocking how loving and close they all were. It took me a while to feel like I belonged and was one of them."

"It did?" I ask, happy to know I'm not a complete weirdo.

"They're all so close. It's hard not to feel like an

outsider, but it's even harder to stay one. They suck you up, and, girl, they never let go." She pats my hand softly before placing her arm across the back of the swing. "The Gallos are the best kind of people."

"They really are. I don't know how I got so lucky."

Suzy smiles. "On paper, Joe and I didn't fit. God, at first, I really didn't want to date the guy, but he was persistent."

"You didn't?"

Hell, I remember the first time I saw Angelo. I wanted him, but I figured he was married and off-limits. I wasn't sure I could even open my heart again, but the big guy had a way of working himself into my soul.

Suzy shakes her head and laughs. "We did sleep together the night we met, but I figured we'd never see each other again."

"Why?"

"Why did I sleep with him, or why did I think we'd never see together?"

"I can see why you slept with him." I laugh softly. "But why did you think you'd never see him again?"

"I was a little naïve and way too innocent for the badass biker that was City."

"City?" I ask.

"That's what his biker buddies call him because he grew up in the big city. The night I met him, my car had broken down on a dark country road, and he pulled over to help me. When he couldn't get the car to start, he offered me a ride to the bar to call for a tow."

"And that turned into you two..."

"Yeah," she says, looking into the distance with a sinful smirk on her face. "I didn't plan on sleeping with him. Hell, he even scared me a bit." She takes another sip of wine as I study her, trying to picture her younger and naïve. "I didn't drink, didn't swear... I was like a nun without the getup. But there I was in this badass biker bar, surrounded by dirty-talkin' rough men, and then I was on the back of his bike. I kind of let myself live a little that night. I'd never had a one-night stand before him, and I assumed we'd sleep together and be done."

"Why?"

"I figured he was a player and the night meant nothing to him. I mean, you've seen him. He's handsome as hell, and the ladies are always eyeing him. I see the way they look at my husband. Even the young ones and I want to punch them in their pretty little faces or their perky, perfect tits."

I let out a howl of laughter. "Somehow, I can't picture that. So, was he a player?"

"He'd only had one long-term relationship before me. He was engaged, but she died tragically before they were married."

My heart aches for him. I know the deep sadness that comes from losing someone you love so completely.

"I could see why he didn't want to settle down for a while after that. When I lost Mitchell, I never thought I'd love again. I figured I'd be an old lady, surrounded by cats, and watching reality television for the rest of my life."

Suzy giggles. "I think City liked the chase. I may have been easy the first night. Don't ever repeat that." She points her finger at me. "But afterward, I tried to put distance between us when other women were throwing themselves at his feet."

"Angelo and I started hanging out as friends, but we flirted a lot. I think we were both still dwelling on our grief so much that we couldn't move forward. But that was what brought us together. Unless you've loved and lost, it's hard to comprehend exactly how the other person feels."

"I can't imagine losing Joe," she says quietly and looks down at her wineglass. "My world would end."

"It feels like that for a long time, but somehow we keep breathing."

"The man may be a total badass and cocky as hell, but he's treated me like a queen since the day I met him. He didn't care that I didn't like to party and I wasn't his usual type. For some reason, we clicked.

God, he even saved my life. How can a girl walk away from a man after he saves her life?"

I gasp. "He did?"

She nods. "Some asshole attacked me in the parking lot of the biker bar. I thought Joe was going to kill him. After that, I knew he'd always protect me. No one had ever done anything even remotely close to that for me. I always only had myself. Not even my parents seemed to give a shit what happened to me."

"The Gallos are very protective," I say, knowing that much about Angelo. The man would take a bullet for me without even blinking.

"They are. Now here I am with three girls, an amazing husband, and a large family that's like a small mob, none of which I planned. It's funny how life works out sometimes."

I don't say anything as I sit next to her, sipping my wine, letting her words seep into my heart.

"What you're feeling is normal," she says like she's reading my mind. "I just wanted to tell you that."

"Thank you for sharing all that with me. I loved hearing about how you and Joe met and fell in love."

"Izzy's story is better." She smirks, and her gaze goes to the window and Izzy. "James was Thomas's best friend."

My eyes widen. "Thomas was okay with that?"

Suzy shakes her head and twists her lips into a salacious smile. "Not at all. It all started at my wedding."

"Wait, I think we need more wine," I tell her and quickly stand. "Don't move."

Everyone's so busy, no one seems to notice me as I run into the dining room, grab a bottle, and head back outside.

Suzy's sitting on the swing, running her fingers through her long blond hair. She holds her glass up and says, "So Thomas sent James to our wedding because he was working so deep undercover, he couldn't make it."

"Okay," I tell her as I fill her glass. "And?"

"I saw the spark as soon as they met. Izzy was Izzy and totally playing it off like she didn't even like the guy. She can be rough sometimes, even on someone as tough as James."

I pour the wine into my glass after I sit down and turn toward Suzy, ready to get the dirt. "Keep going."

"She got totally shit-faced and ended up in his hotel room doing the nasty all night, and then she left without even saying goodbye. Just dropped the guy like a hot potato."

"How did they get together again?"

"Izzy went to Bike Week and got in over her head. Thomas was there, still undercover, but somehow, he got a message to James and had Izzy arrested for drug possession."

My mouth's hanging open, but she continues.

"After she was arrested, James went to the station and decided to bring her home."

"That's all it took?"

Suzy laughs loudly, slapping her leg. "No way. James wasn't going to play nice with her, so he handcuffed her to the bed all night and most of the way home."

"He did not." My eyes widen.

"Izzy was not amused."

I suck my lips into my mouth, trying not to laugh because more than one person has turned their attention to the window, and I like our little Suzy and Tilly bubble. "So, what happened?"

Suzy shrugs. "It seems James likes the chase as much as Joe. And for some reason, that man can bring Izzy to her knees, and I'm not talking figuratively either." Suzy waggles her eyebrows. "He's straight up hot as fuck when he's being all Dom and bossy. I've never seen anyone tame Izzy the way he does, still to this day."

"I want to know all the stories. Tell me about Mike and Mia, Anthony and Max, and Thomas and Angel."

"Girl, Angel and Thomas are a whole other story. It's a wild one too."

"I feel like I need to know everything."

Suzy raises her glass, touching it lightly to mine. "I'll tell you everything."

An hour later, the bottle of wine is gone, and we're both giggling like college girls who've never drunk before. The stories Suzy told me had me laughing my ass off, and the wine didn't help me keep my shit under control.

"You ladies okay out here?" Angelo asks as he pops his head out the front door. "You've been out here awhile."

"We're perfect," Suzy tells him. "Just girl talk and sharing a bit of family history."

Angelo's eyes linger on my face, and when he sees my tears are from laughter, a smile spreads across his lips. "Okay. Don't get too drunk. You two want anything?"

"Privacy," Suzy says easily. "We have some things that aren't meant for a man's ears."

"Enough said." Angelo puts up a hand and disappears.

"I know he thought we were talking about periods or something. It's where a man's mind automatically goes and scares the bejesus out of them. Doesn't take much more than the mere thought, and they vanish quickly."

I giggle louder. "Thank you for tonight, Suzy. I

really needed some laughter, and your telling me all your stories helped me feel like I'm part of something bigger."

She places her hand on mine. "Sweetheart, you're a Gallo now. You are part of something special."

I feel it deep in my bones. There's something magical about being part of a family, having a tribe to call your own. I no longer feel like an outsider after being clued in on everyone and every crazy, sexy detail. I am now, and forever shall be, a Gallo.

CHAPTER TWENTY

ANGELO

"That was ridiculously fast." Vinnie wraps his arm around his new wife's middle and pulls her close to his side. "It took us longer to drive there than for the entire ceremony."

"The next one will be longer," Bianca tells him as she rests her head on his arm and walks toward the pizza place. "But it doesn't matter. I'm officially Mrs. Vincent Gallo." She holds up her hand and stares at the ring as its light splinters in the setting sun.

"You made me the happiest man in the world today," he tells her.

Tilly looks up at me, our hands linked, and smiles. She's been like an entirely different person since her talk with Suzy last night. I'm not sure what they said, but whatever it was, it changed her.

"You ready for this?" Tilly calls out before Bianca and Vinnie make it to the front door.

Bianca stops and turns, taking a deep breath. "Let's just hope my dad doesn't lose his shit. The last thing we need is someone getting arrested."

"You think that'll happen?" Tilly's mouth falls open.

Bianca shrugs. "Hopefully my parents will be happy. But my father has a temper, and I don't know how they'll feel about me being pregnant."

"Maybe we shouldn't tell them that," Vinnie says as his shoulders tense. "We can wait."

I slap him on the back, trying to knock some sense into him. "Stop the bullshit. We'll all be here. Nothing will happen. Just tell the old man and give him a few minutes to realize he's going to be a grandfather."

Tilly stares at the happy couple. "Do your parents know we're here to celebrate you two getting married?"

Bianca shakes her head. "Nope. It's going to be like a one-two punch."

"Oh, lordie," Tilly whispers and bites her bottom lip.

"Yep. It might get a little out of hand." Vinnie grimaces for a moment before pulling his lips into a tight smile. "But at least everything will be out in the open."

We'll add this day to the list of dumb shit Vinnie's done in his life. They should've been honest about the baby to begin with. I'm pretty sure my mother is going to go apeshit when she finds out about the shotgun wedding. Her anger won't have anything to do with the wedding not taking place in a church, but the fact that she wasn't there to witness the blessed event.

"Last chance to run," I tease as he reaches for the door handle, and Tilly swats my chest.

"Stop. Leave them be. It'll all be fine."

She thinks so, which is cute, but I've met many men like Mr. Hernandez, and I can say it won't be fine. He's going to go crazy, probably close to nuclear, when he hears his baby girl is knocked up and they snuck away to get married at city hall instead of in a church and before God.

I lean down and kiss Tilly's cheek. "I'll remind you of that in a half hour."

"Let's do this, baby," Vinnie says to Bianca, ushering her through the door.

Half the pizza shop is filled with family. Everyone's here, including Bianca's parents, grandmother, and brothers who look a little out of place and overly curious about why they've been asked to attend a dinner at a restaurant they probably wouldn't normally be caught dead in.

It takes ten minutes to say hello, including hugs and kisses. That's the rub of an Italian family. Hellos and goodbyes take forever.

"Why are we here, Bianca?" her mother asks as soon as the family starts to settle back into their seats.

Bianca turns to Vinnie, twisting her hands in front of herself, and gives him a nervous smile. "You say it," she says softly. "I can't."

"What's wrong? Are you hurt? Sick?" Her mother's gaze roams Bianca's body, and I can see the worry on her face.

"No, Mom. I'm not sick," Bianca says quickly, but it does nothing to alleviate the tension.

Tilly squeezes my hand and leans over. "This is going to be intense, isn't it?"

"Maybe they'll take it well, like you said," I tell her, but I know it's complete bullshit.

"Then what is it? Why are we all here?"

Vinnie steps forward, his hand linked with Bianca's as his eyes move across the room. "Bianca and I have an announcement to make."

Bianca's mother quickly does the sign of the cross,

touching her head, heart, and each shoulder. Bianca's father's hand is already clenched so tightly, I'm pretty sure he's about ready to pop.

"Spit it out, guys. You're killing us!" Mike yells out, but he knows everything. The parents are the only ones in the dark.

Vinnie holds out Bianca's hand, showing off the ring. "Bianca and I were married today."

The people not in the know, my parents and Bianca's family, all gasp with wide eyes. The rest of the family, my cousins and siblings, all start clapping and hollering for the happy couple.

Bianca's father stands straight up, hand still curled in a fist. "You what?"

"We got married at city hall, Papa."

Bianca's father's eyes slice to his wife, but she's too busy crying, and I'm not sure they're entirely tears of joy either.

"How could you do this to your mother?"

Tilly's eyes find mine, and I cringe because this isn't going as happily as Vinnie and Bianca hoped, and they haven't even dropped the biggest bomb yet.

"We couldn't wait," Vinnie says, not giving one shit that her dad is mad.

"We'll still get married in the church. We'll renew our vows before God, Papa."

"The green-eyed one," Bianca's grandmother says with a big smile. "I knew. I always knew."

"How could you not tell us or, hell, invite us to the ceremony?" her father seethes.

Bianca's grandmother reaches up and grabs her son's hand. "Calm down, my son. She's with child. This is a celebration."

Bianca's father's head jerks back at his mother-in-law's words. "She is not. She can't be." He turns his narrowed eyes toward Bianca and Vinnie. "Are you?"

"Surprise," Bianca exclaims, waving her hands in the air like she's trying to make light of the situation.

"Should we take cover?" Tilly whispers in my ear.

"I don't know, sweetheart. Just keep still and see what happens. I think the old woman has it covered."

"How could you?" Bianca's dad asks.

The grandmother tightens her grip on his arm. "Sit down," she tells him, and there's no missing the agitation in her tone. "You will not ruin this happy day."

His lip curls in a snarl. "Happy? How is this happy? My little girl is knocked up and got married at city hall because she's carrying his child."

"This is fate. I saw it many years ago, just as I saw you for my daughter."

"You're going to have a baby?" Bianca's mother asks like she's just coming out of shock.

"Yes, Mama. I'm so sorry," Bianca tells her from a safe distance away.

Her mother rises and wipes the tears from her face as she walks around the table and approaches her daughter.

"Should I go to Bianca in case something bad happens?" Tilly asks, but I shake my head.

Bianca's mother reaches out, cradling her daughter's face in her hand. "My baby's going to have a baby?"

"Yes," Bianca says with watery eyes. "Don't be mad, Mama. We're so happy. So very happy."

"I'm going to be a grandmother?" she asks again like she's still in disbelief.

Bianca nods. "You are."

A smile spreads across her mother's face. "You've made me very happy, little girl. So very happy."

"You're okay with this?" her father asks.

Bianca's mother turns her attention toward her husband for a moment. "Yes, Grandpa, I am. Do not ruin this day for our daughter. Do not taint her pregnancy like your mother did mine."

That is enough to shut him up as he sits back down and unclenches his fist, but he keeps his eyes focused on Vinnie.

"You're not mad at me, Mama?" Bianca swallows, trying to hold the smile on her face.

"A life is never anything to be mad about, child. You have a good man, a loving husband, and you're both giving me the greatest gift ever."

I finally let out a long breath I didn't even realize I'd been holding. "Well, that wasn't so bad."

"I told you so," Tilly says and elbows me in the side.

"I'm going to be a grandmother again," my mother says, having been uncharacteristically quiet until now. "This is the best week ever."

The news of the pregnancy, along with the wedding, causes another round of hugs and kisses. At this rate, we'll never eat.

Suzy leans over to Tilly. "Tonight, you tell me how everyone here got together. I want to know all the dirt."

Tilly winks at her. "Girl, I have you covered."

"Are you two gossiping?" I ask, nuzzling my face into my wife's neck.

"It's not gossip if it's true." Tilly smirks.

"We have so much to plan," Bianca's mother says as she takes her seat next to her still shell-shocked husband. "We must have you married before God, plan the christening, and your baby shower, of course."

"We have time for that, Mama."

Vinnie pulls out a chair for his wife and takes the seat next to her at the extremely long table filled with two families and many generations. The kids are at another table, a small army on their own.

Something about tonight, sitting at the pizza place we spent time in as kids, feels right. I haven't felt this at peace in so long, the sensation is almost foreign. The calm among the chaos I grew up with is back, and for the first time in a long time, anything seems possible.

CHAPTER TWENTY-ONE

TILLY

B<small>ETTY IS STANDING IN THE KITCHEN, SPOON IN</small> hand, trying to replicate her sister-in-law's sauce recipe. "I swear to God, she left something out." She grimaces as she takes a small sip of the red sauce from a spoon. "It's too bitter."

"Try adding a little sugar. It'll help cut the acidity."

Betty smiles, and Angelo puts his arms around my waist, nuzzling my neck. "Do you need a break?" he whispers.

I turn my face, staring into his beautiful eyes. "From your mom? Never."

She may be a lot to handle sometimes, but she's

Betty and now my mother too. It had been so long since I'd had someone to call Mom that I don't really care how over the top or crazy she is sometimes, she's still mine.

"I can hear you," Betty says, and when I look up, I see the smile on her face.

"Go back to the living room with the men," she tells him, waving the spoon around in front of her. "Send your sisters in here because I'm sure they need a break from all the testosterone by now."

"Fine, Ma. I'll tell them," he murmurs against my skin before he's gone.

"How's the shop doing since you've been busy all week?" Betty asks, grabbing a small bowl of sugar and sprinkling a little into the pot.

"A little more," I tell her. "It's going fine. I have a solid team working there and hired a fabulous pastry chef so I don't have to be chained to the bakery."

"Smart girl." Betty winks at me. "Life is hectic. Throw in two kids, a husband, and a business, and time passes in a blur. Just make sure to take some time and enjoy every minute you can. Soon enough, you'll be older and looking back, wishing you could do things over again."

I move next to her and grab a clean spoon, dipping it into the sauce and focus on my mother-in-law. "I know how precious time is, Ma. I promise not to take a moment for granted."

She reaches out and cups my cheek. "That's my girl."

I smile, feeling like I am hers. She's the only mother I have, and I wouldn't trade her for anyone in the world. I place the spoon in my mouth, and my lips pucker around the spoon. "More sugar," I whisper, trying to swallow down the strong tomato taste lingering on my tongue.

"We're here," Daphne says with Delilah and Bianca at her side. "What's up?"

"Sit," Betty tells them, dumping more sugar into the pot. "I just want some company and some girl talk. We've been so busy this week, I haven't had time to catch up with my girls."

"Grab another bottle of red," Daphne tells Delilah and pulls down four wineglasses from the cabinet. "And a bottle of water for Bianca."

"I can have a few sips," Bianca says as she sits down on the stool across the island. "My doctor said it was okay but not to overdo it."

"I drank while I was pregnant," Betty replies.

"That explains what happened." Daphne chuckles.

"Oh, stop. All my children are healthy and happy. What more could a mother ask for?" Betty dumps a few boxes of pasta into the boiling water and stares at us across the island. "I have everything I ever wanted."

"Is there anything you'd change if you could?" Delilah asks Betty.

"I'd have more children."

"Oh Jesus," Daphne mutters. "Life was crazy with the four of us. I can't imagine more."

"Would you rather have been an only child?" Betty asks Daphne.

"Trust me, it sucks," I add.

"It totally does," Delilah says.

Daphne shrugs. "I guess not, but having three brothers tried my nerves sometimes."

"I never wanted my children to feel what I did," Betty says as she leans against the counter, crosses her arms, and bows her head.

"Ma," Daphne whispers and covers her mouth.

Betty shakes her head. "I had a brother."

The room is silent besides the garbled voices from the family room. My eyes are locked on Betty, and I see the pain etched on her face.

Daphne's out of her seat, making her way around the island. "Ma, you don't have to talk about this."

Betty moves to her daughter and grabs her hands. "It's important for you to hear this." Betty turns to us, still holding Daphne's hands. "For all of you to hear this."

I brace myself because I know whatever she's going to say is going to gut me. Utterly and completely wreck me in a way I hadn't expected for a simple family dinner.

"It was important for me to have a lot of children. Growing up, I had a brother, Davin. He was older by a handful of years, but we were still close. I never once thought about life without him. I thought he'd always be there, you know?" She wipes the corner of her eyes with the back of her finger. "He had the most beautiful smile, and he was quite the ladies' man. He just had one of those personalities where people were drawn to him." She smiles, but her eyes hold nothing but sorrow. "When I was sixteen, Davin was out with his friends late at night. He did this often, but I remember waking in the middle of the night to my mother screaming downstairs. It's a sound I'll never forget."

I'm frozen to my seat, unable to move as I stare at Betty and soak in her pain.

"In that moment, I went from having a brother to being an only child."

My vision blurs in her sadness. I feel it in my heart and my gut so completely.

"Ma, you still have a brother," Daphne tells her.

"He was born, but he's no longer here," Betty replies and squeezes Daphne's hands. "My life never felt the same after that. I was so lost. I felt like everything I was changed in that moment. The only person who knew my secrets, my inside jokes had vanished. I never had a day without Davin in it until then. I didn't know life without him."

I wipe away my tears and bite my lip, trying to stop myself from sobbing. Delilah and Bianca are doing the same. None of us have heard Betty talk about her brother, what happened, or how it affected her. She rarely talks about her family, and I understand why. Her parents and only sibling have died. The pain she must feel even now, decades later, is so deep, it's not something she can easily vocalize.

"When I had Angelo and looked at his sweet little face, I knew I never wanted him to experience the same pain I had. I knew I wanted lots of children because I never wanted my child to know how it felt being part of something amazing and then having nothing."

Daphne pulls her mother into her arms and buries her face in her neck. "Ma, I'm so sorry."

"I would've had ten kids if my body was able and your father would've kept his ass out of jail a little more. I never want you to have that hurt."

"I won't," Daphne tells her as she rubs Betty's back.

"I know you won't, baby. I made sure of that, and now you have sisters." Betty moves out of Daphne's embrace. "You have a large family filled with love and children of your own. You all have one another, and that's all that matters. There's nothing more precious than family. I want you all to understand that too. There's nothing more precious than the people you surround yourself with, both through marriage and blood. I never want anything to come between you girls and my boys."

I understand exactly what she's saying. The sting and ache I felt when Mitchell died were excruciating, and the only person who got me through those moments was Roger. He was the only family I had until I met Angelo. I'm not sure I would've survived without him.

"You can never have too many people in your life who love you. Remember that," Betty says, dabbing her eyes with her fingers.

"We know," Daphne says.

"I can never begin to imagine your heartache of losing your brother, Betty," I say.

"Ma," she reminds me.

I nod. "Ma. But I promise nothing is more important to me than my family. You girls..." I pause and collect my thoughts for a moment, trying to get my lip to stop trembling, but I fail and continue. "You gave me something I never had. Not even when I had a different life, I never had this." I wave my hands toward the four women in front of me. "I never had a family that I felt had my back all the time. And not just a little family, but a big one so full of love and happiness that I ask myself every day how I got so damn lucky."

Betty smiles and reaches across the island to pat my hand. "We're the blessed ones, sweetheart. You brought my baby back to life at a time I wasn't sure he'd ever be like he was."

I want to argue with her because I didn't know the Angelo before, but I knew the Tilly before Angelo. Although I'm living, thriving, and completely in love, I know I'm not the woman I used to be. The pain has a way of staying etched on your heart forever. The wound may close, but the scar will always remain as a constant reminder of the path I walked and the hurt I endured.

"We'll always have each other," Delilah says. "I've never been so loved. I don't know where I'd be without this family." Delilah lets out a relieved sigh. "I'm happy I'll never have to know either."

Daphne smiles. "We're a sisterhood."

Bianca nods. "I always wanted a sister, and I can't even begin to tell you how happy I am to finally have girls at my side." She places her hands on her stomach. "My baby is going to have some kick-ass aunts and an amazing and strong grandma."

"My children and grandchildren will never know

what it means to be alone, and for that, I'm thankful. Even though I had to go through the hurt, I'm okay with taking that if it means I've shielded them from the same pain."

"You have, Ma," Daphne says and wraps her arms around her mother's waist. "We will never be alone, and neither will you."

There are heavy footsteps behind us, and I turn, catching the men, our men, standing near the doorway to the kitchen. They're watching us, eyes roaming around the room, taking in the teary-eyed faces of their women.

"Do you need us to give you time?" Angelo asks, but he's not asking me; he's asking his mother.

She shakes her head. "No, sweetheart, but can you boys set the table? The food is just about ready."

Angelo nods and makes his way into the room and toward me. "You okay?" he whispers as he leans forward to kiss me.

"Perfect, baby." I smile, moving into him and wanting that kiss.

It's sweet and short, soft and warm, but as he pulls away, his eyes search mine. "You sure you're okay?"

I nod and smile. "I couldn't be better."

"I love you," he whispers.

"I love you too," I whisper back.

And I couldn't be better. I have everything I ever

wanted. A great husband, loving children, parents, sisters and brothers, and most of all, love. I'll never know the pain of being alone again like I felt after my parents died. I knew sadness, but in this moment, I am certain I'll never be alone again. I am part of something bigger, a family that has taken me in like I have been there my entire life, and for that, I'll be forever thankful.

CHAPTER TWENTY-TWO

TILLY

One Year Later

S<small>UZY'S</small> <small>THE FIRST ONE TO ME, WITH HER ARMS</small> outstretched, waiting just beyond security at the Tampa airport. "Lemme see those cheeks."

I turn my face, making a joke, because I know she isn't talking about me. "They've grown since the last time you saw me."

She waves her hand at me with a giggle and

reaches for the wide-eyed baby in my arms. "I'm a sucker for a chubby baby."

I hand my son to Suzy and am thankful to give my arms a break. "Well, Mason most certainly is that."

"Oh, he's a heavy little thing." Suzy cradles him in her arms, running her nose along his head, getting the great baby smell I've grown all too fond of myself.

"Mommy," Brax says at my side, yanking on my top when I don't react fast enough.

"Yes, sweetheart?"

"Carry me," he says and raises his arms in the air, wiggling them for effect. "Please."

I lift Brax, who is almost too big to be carried, especially by me, but the transition with the new baby hasn't been easy on the kids. They've taken it in stride, each day growing fonder of the little guy who keeps waking them up in the middle of the night. "Sure, baby." I kiss his cheek.

Tate's in Angelo's arms, where she usually is now that Mason has arrived. When she isn't in his arms, she's pretending to be Mason's mommy, which is adorable. She's been such a good helper the last two months.

I take a moment to look around as I settle Brax on my hip, ready for the long haul to baggage claim. The entire Gallo family is standing in the middle of the main terminal, holding signs, flowers, and balloons, welcoming us to Florida.

Before they left Chicago, they made us promise we'd come to Tampa to attend Gigi's graduation and spend a little time in their world like they did in ours.

It is a much-needed break after a long and gloomy Chicago winter. I've missed the thick, damp air of the South and the endless streams of sunshine.

"Hand her over, kid," Izzy says to Bianca, taking Amelia from her arms without hesitation. "God, this almost makes me sad I'll never have another little one."

James pulls his wife closer, staring down at the doe-eyed little bundle in Izzy's arms. "We can try for another. Maybe the next one will be a girl."

Izzy's face tips upward to her husband, and she narrows her eyes. "Don't get any ideas. I'm way beyond the baby stage, and I'm not about to start over. Plus, we both know I'm cursed to forever have boys, but at least I have nieces to spoil."

"It's always better when it's someone else's kid." James laughs and kisses Izzy's cheek before turning his attention to the dark-haired beauty in his wife's arms. "She's absolutely perfect."

The put-together Vinnie and Bianca have vanished. The months of not sleeping and parenthood have taken their toll on the young couple.

"You can keep her for a few nights," Vinnie says to

Izzy. "I could use some rest and time alone with my woman."

Izzy looks to James, and he nods. "That's a deal. Only a few nights so you kids can sleep," she tells them.

"Oh, thank God. I'm so tired from traveling, and I'm not sure I could take another sleepless night," Vinnie says, running his fingers through his already messy hair.

I'm thankful for Angelo. Although I'm a first-time mother and worry about every little thing, he's calm, cool, and collected with this being his third child. The family has rallied around Vinnie and Bianca, helping in every way we can, but I can see the wear and tear on their faces.

Everyone's busy hugging and kissing, the usual Gallo family hello that I've grown accustomed to. I would expect nothing less.

"Let's get the bags and head back," Uncle Sal says, corralling us all toward the escalators.

Lucio and Delilah walk in front of me. Lulu's in Lucio's arms, playing with his cheeks, and Zoe's in Delilah's arms with her head on her mom's shoulder, fast asleep.

Leo's carrying Nino as he clutches his teddy bear tight to his body, and Daphne's walking at their side. I hold Angelo's hand as we descend the escalators to a busy baggage claim area, and I'm thankful the family has come here to help with the kids and the mountain of luggage, car seats, and strollers we checked back in Chicago.

Thirty minutes later, we're out of the airport and piled into their SUVs. "I can't thank you enough for getting us," I say to Suzy as we make our way down the highway toward their town.

"We wouldn't miss this for the world," she says, turning around in her seat to face me. "It's been too long since we've seen each other."

"You sure you guys don't want to stay with us?" Joe asks, glancing in the rearview mirror as he follows the entourage of cars in front of us.

"I'm sure. You have enough going on, and it's not easy with infants. We'll be fine at the hotel. Thankfully, they had suites, so we won't be jammed into a little space."

"I'm thinking we can do the beach tomorrow," Suzy says, changing the subject.

I grimace at the thought of putting on a bathing suit because I haven't been able to shake all my baby weight. "I don't know."

Her gaze follows my hands as I cover my stomach. "Oh no, you don't. Your body is kick-ass. And let me let you in on a little secret—this isn't Baywatch."

"What?" I giggle.

"It's not all tight bodies, big tits, and hot guys. This is Florida. You have a better chance of seeing an old man with a beer gut wearing a Speedo on the beach than some hot young thing."

"You're really selling me here, Suzy."

I remember vacationing in the Panhandle as a kid with my parents. They loved the beach, and it was only a few hours' drive from home. We went every year to the same hotel and sat on the same stretch of sand, watching the waves from the Gulf of Mexico.

"You'll see. We have a few big portable canopies for the kids to play under, so they don't get burned, and another one for the adults, especially those of you who haven't seen sunshine in months."

"I'm getting really sick of the cold and snow. This trip couldn't have come at a better time." I smile and grab Angelo's hand. "We needed this."

"You should just move here," Joe says like it's a simple thing to do.

"It's not that easy," Angelo says. But I can see it in his eyes; he's as sick of the shitty, gray winters of the North as I am.

"You guys can sell the bar and open one down here if you need something to do. I'm sure after a week in the sunshine, no one's going to want to go back."

"You're probably right." Angelo squeezes my hand.

"Your parents are getting older, and before the kids get too old, it's an easier move."

Suzy's practically buzzing in her seat. "Oh my God. That would be the best thing in the world. Imagine all the Sunday dinners and the holidays... What could be more perfect?"

Angelo and I have talked about moving south, giving our kids a better quality of life outside the big city. I'd love our kids to have something I never did—a big family to spoil them and shower them with love.

"It's something we've discussed. I'm sure it won't take too much convincing to get everyone to move here," Angelo tells Joe.

I stare out the windows, watching the endless green grass pass by us in a blur and the palm trees swaying in the breeze. There're no tall buildings and cement for as far as the eye can see like in Chicago.

"It's really beautiful here," I say as we get farther away from the airport and more into the country.

"Life is slower here," Joe says. "I don't miss the rat race in Chicago."

"I've missed the South," I say softly, unable to take my eyes off the landscape.

Joe and Angelo talk most of the way home as I stare out the window, thinking about what it would be like to live here, surrounded by the Gallos. I can't imagine anything better, and I want that for our children.

An hour later, our luggage is dropped off at the hotel, and we're driving down the driveway to Joe and Suzy's place. My mouth drops open as soon as I see what looks like a mansion nestled in the woods.

"You live here?" I whisper in disbelief with my face between the two front seats, unable to tear my gaze away from its beauty.

"Yes, living here is so much cheaper than Chicago. You could probably get something like this with how much your place is worth up there."

There're lush trees and green grass everywhere surrounding the grand structure that looks like it was plucked from a mountaintop.

"You've done well for yourself, cousin," Angelo says.

I turn to look at him, and I can see the awe on his face as I mouth *oh my God.* "How many acres do you have?"

"Fifteen and the place next to us is for sale, which I think is about ten acres. And the house is even more spectacular," Joe says, but the hint isn't subtle.

"I'm sure everyone is starving and ready for a cold drink," Suzy says as the SUV comes to a slow stop.

"Sweet tea?" I'm hopeful. Although Chicago is known for their cuisine, the sweet tea there is nothing like the real Southern version.

"Of course." She giggles. "I fresh brewed some just for you."

"I've died and gone to heaven." I'm being overdramatic, but I don't care.

I'm happy as hell to be in the South, in the sun, and among family again.

Everyone's out of the cars quickly, the kids running around the yard as Aunt Maria and Aunt Fran stand on the front porch, watching over the kids.

"This place is crazy," Lucio says to us as he grabs Lulu from the car seat and sets her on the ground. "Did they tell you we should move here?"

Angelo nods. "There were words."

"I think we should do it. We'll be too old soon to drop everything and head south."

"But what about the bar?" Angelo asks as we walk up the driveway.

"We can sell the bar." Lucio shrugs. "Do you really want to be a bartender your entire life?"

"We have Vinnie and Leo to consider," Angelo replies.

My shoulders slump a little because we can't leave them behind, and I'm not sure Vinnie could easily move now that he's the franchise player in Chicago. Then there's Leo and his hotel empire, which has its headquarters in Chicago.

"Vinnie doesn't work the entire year, and most of

the players don't actually live in Chicago anyway. Leo, he's the boss, the headquarters can move with him, or he can do most of his work remotely. He's often out of town anyway. His life wouldn't change all that much," Lucio says.

"Let's talk about this later as a family," I tell the boys because this is a decision we must make together.

That's what I've learned about the Gallos. They don't make big decisions as individuals. They're a package deal.

Where one goes, they all follow.

CHAPTER TWENTY-THREE

ANGELO

I CRAWL UNDER THE THIN SHEETS, CURLING MY body into my girl. "Are the kids asleep?" she asks.

My hand is around her waist, just below her breasts. "They are," I say against her neck before running my tongue along her soft skin and sliding my thumb underneath the swell of her breast.

"What if they wake up?" Her voice is all breathy and wanton as she pushes her ass into my hard-on.

"They didn't nap, and with all the travel and excitement, no one will wake up for a little while."

She moves onto her back, staring up at me in the faint glow from the television. "What if they catch us?"

"Baby." I smirk, loving this woman so damn much. "We can live dangerously." My gaze drops to her lush lips as she bites the bottom one, working the soft skin between her teeth. "Let go a little bit. Stop thinking so much," I tell her.

"They could wake up and see something."

I'm out of the bed and at the door that separates our room from the living room, where our three kids are fast asleep. I close it quietly and lock it before turning around, catching Tilly checking out my bare ass.

"You seriously have an amazing ass. It's so not fair."

"You got the more impressive set of tits, so let's not complain who got the better end of that deal," I tell her as I slide back into the bed next to her, pulling the sheet down to expose her body.

She shakes her breasts right in my face, knowing exactly what she's doing and how she affects me. "You'd look funny with these."

Grabbing her around the waist, I pull her closer to my side. I run a finger down the space between her breasts, slowly raking it back and forth as I stare into her eyes. "They're mine. Make no doubt about that."

"Sweetheart," Tilly says, reaching down and fisting my cock. "I need you inside me."

My body jerks with each stroke, and I need to be inside her too. "Don't you want to take it slow?" I graze my fingertip over her nipple, and her eyes darken as her grip tightens.

"I want you between my thighs."

And being a good husband, I go there. Sliding between her thighs, hovering over her naked skin, and staring down at her. "Better?" I ask, taunting her with my cock just out of reach.

The look in her eyes is anything but amused. "Angelo."

"Baby," I reply, but as soon as her mouth opens to complain, I lean forward and pull her nipple between my lips, silencing her.

Her fingers are in my hair, nails against my scalp, making my skin break out in goose bumps. She moans as I suck harder, drawing the stiff peak deeper into my mouth. I love the way she says my name and claws at my skin when I'm loving her.

She wraps her legs around my body and sticks her heels into my ass. "Fuck me," she whispers.

I'm done playing games. Done playing around. When you have three sleeping kids in the next room, there isn't time for any bullshit but getting busy and making love to my woman.

With a small thrust of my hips, her legs fall away, spreading for me. Inch by inch, I slide inside her until there's no more left to give. She pulls my face forward, pressing her lips to mine, and kisses me deeply. Not just deep, but with so much hunger and need, I can taste the sweetness on her tongue.

My movements are slow but powerful, careful not to make too much noise, because if any of the kids wake up right now, everything will be ruined. I can't risk it. There's not enough space between us and them. The walls aren't thick enough to really pound my wife, but I take things slow and gentle.

With one hand in my hair and the other on my ass, she pulls me forward every time I pull out, forcing me back in. Thrust after thrust, we're both covered in a fine sheen of sweat and panting into each other's mouth and right on the edge of ecstasy. Then I thrust harder, forcing her body upward with the movement just like she likes it. But it's wrong. It's not enough to get her off. I know her body well enough to know when she's in the groove and I'm hitting the right spot, and I'm not.

The bed isn't right. The need to be quiet isn't right, and that leaves only one thing to do. I slide my arm behind her back and move toward the floor, carrying her against me with our mouths still locked.

She's in my lap, my cock still buried deep when I murmur against her lips. "Ride me, baby. Ride me hard."

There's no need to be soft and gentle when we're on the floor. There's no squeaky headboard or loud mattress, setting off an alarm to the kids that it's time to interrupt our pleasure before it's finished.

Those words are all Tilly needs to hear before she arches her back and she's riding me like she's at a rodeo on the wildest bull in the ring. Her lips aren't on mine anymore. Her mouth's open, gasping for air as she pounds into me, riding my cock so hard, I can't do anything but stare at her beauty and enjoy the ride.

My ass aches from the thin carpet and cement, but there's no way I'm stopping what she's doing. The pleasure on my cock outweighs any pain in my ass. And within minutes, she's moaning with her mouth closed as my lips close around her nipple and tip her over the edge. I'm with her, shaking with the orgasm and fighting for breath. She drops her head forward onto my shoulder, and I wrap my arms around her, holding our sticky bodies together tightly. I don't know how long we sit like this, skin-on-skin, wet, heaving, but it's long enough that my legs have gone numb, though you won't find my ass complaining.

"Would you really want to live here?" she asks in the silence.

"Would you?"

I couldn't care less where I live. All I need is my family. You could throw me in the middle of fucking nowhere, and I'd be fine as long as my wife and kids were there with me.

"I miss the South," she says quietly, turning her head so her lips are at my neck.

"If you want the South, you get the South."

"But there's the bar, and the bakery has really taken off."

"We can sell them both, start something new here, something together if you want."

"It's a big decision."

I tighten my hold on her back, brushing my lips against her shoulder. "Whatever you want to do, I want to do. I don't care about anything else except for being with you, babe."

She leans back, taking her shoulder from my lips. "You think anyone else would move here?"

I shrug. "I don't know. They were talking about it at Joe's. No one gave a hard no. They're probably all in their rooms, talking about it now like we are."

"The kids would love it here," she sighs. "It's just so much to think about. Moving an entire family is a big undertaking and an even bigger risk."

"Sweetheart, we have plenty of money. We could go years without having a job and still live pretty damn well. We can hire movers, sell the businesses, and get out of dodge before shit gets even worse."

The shit I'm referring to is the violence in the city. Back in the day, it used to be the mafia shooting it out on the streets of Chicago. But now, it's all about the gangs. There are so many innocent bystanders being killed, it makes my heart ache. The last thing I want is my kids growing up in an area where it's too dangerous for them to play outside and just be fucking kids.

"We'll see what everyone thinks tomorrow. I have a feeling after the shitty winter we just had, they're more than ready to blow town. I don't see much downside to living here."

"There're hurricanes." She cringes. "They can be awful too. Nothing quite as scary as those winds for hours upon hours."

"At least you see them coming, unlike a stray bullet from some asshat's gun."

"You have a point."

"We don't need to make a decision tonight. Let's think about it and what we want for our future. We decide as a family, and either way shit works out, I'm good as long as I've got you and my babies with me."

She smiles when I say that.

"Now, I want to hold my woman, skin on skin, and go to sleep."

"Sweetheart." She touches my cheek. "I can't sleep naked in a hotel, and you know the baby's going to wake up too. So, you can have some leg-on-leg action and maybe an arm, but nothing else."

"I hate hotels," I grumble under my breath.

She untangles herself from my body and heads

toward the suitcase, pulling out a long T-shirt and panties. "It's just for a week. You'll survive."

I throw myself onto the bed and put my arm under my head, letting my gaze travel up those long, muscular legs. "You're looking fine in my shirt, babe."

She curls into my side, her head on my shoulder and hand on my chest. "Don't get any ideas, mister."

I run my fingers down her arm that's resting on my chest. "Sleep, sweetheart. I wasn't getting any ideas, just complimenting my woman and knowing I'm the luckiest son of a bitch in the world."

She tips her head and smiles. "I love you."

"I love you too." I tip my head downward and kiss her lips. "Now, sleep."

She's out a few minutes later, almost like a narcoleptic since the baby arrived. She's exhausted, trying to run the bakery, be mom of the year, and settle into a new routine that revolves around three kids instead of two.

I think a move south where the living is slow and easy is just what we need. I know my girl would thrive here. She'd kick up her feet, relax a little, and maybe enjoy life a little more.

CHAPTER TWENTY-FOUR

TILLY

"What are you doing?" I ask Izzy when I find her near the corner of the house, staring down the driveway.

She glances at me for a moment with a scowl before returning her attention to the front of the house. "Watching this clusterfuck finally explode."

I lean into her, sneaking a peek, and see Gigi and who I assume is Keith, although I've never met him, standing in the driveway. From the way her arms are flying and the look on his face, I don't think the words they're exchanging are pretty.

Keith is cute. He has the surfer boy look nailed,

with the floppy hair covering his eyes, tanned skin, and swimmer's build. Although he's handsome, from what I know about him, he sounds like a complete asshole.

"She's finally doing it," Izzy whispers. She hasn't moved. Her eyes are glued to the couple. "She's finally kicking that loser to the curb."

My eyes widen, and my mouth hangs open. "But it's her graduation party. That's so sad."

I couldn't imagine losing my boyfriend on the day I graduated, celebrating and partying with my family and friends.

"Tilly, it's not sad," she whispers.

"Maybe we should give them privacy," I whisper back.

"Shush. I can't hear."

I guess there's no such thing as privacy on this side of the family, which is really no different from Angelo's family. Everybody is in each other's business. Secrets are almost nonexistent, and if you dare to utter something you don't want shared, you do it inside your house and not at a family dinner or the bar where the likelihood of being overheard is high.

Gigi steps forward, getting right in Keith's face. "I fucking saw you. Don't lie to me!" she screams.

"You saw nothing!" he yells back as his eyes narrow.

"Oh shit," Izzy says, and my breathing falters.

This is some heavy shit for two kids. I don't care if they're eighteen and just graduated from high school, they're still kids with so much to learn and experience.

"I can't watch," I whisper and move to walk away, but Izzy grabs my wrist and holds me there.

"Stay," she tells me and grips my wrist tight. "She may need backup."

"Maybe we should get her daddy."

"No. No men allowed."

Gigi clenches her hands at her sides. "I'm done, Keith. We're over. We were planning to be over by now anyway. Let's just end it tonight. The last person I want in my life right now is someone who's a liar and a cheat."

"I'm not a fucking liar or a cheat," he barks.

"They sure have some mouths on them," I whisper, which earns me the evil eye from Izzy.

When Keith reaches for her arm, Gigi twists, escaping his hold. Her entire body is moving as her hand rears back, and she lunges forward, smacking him clear across the face. His head snaps to the side, and he's slow to look at her again, but when he does, there's nothing but hatred and anger.

"You're a worthless bitch, Gigi. All high and mighty with your V-card still intact. What the fuck was I supposed to do? Wait for you? I'm a fucking man, and I have needs."

My eyes widen. "Oh lord."

"No shit," Izzy whispers and starts to move toward them, but now it's my turn to hold her back.

"Don't go. Wait. Shouldn't we let her handle it?"

Izzy shakes her head. "You're right. She's really a badass chick. She knows how to fight and fend off douchebags like him."

"I'm so glad I didn't sleep with you, Keith. I hope you're happy with Amber. You don't deserve my pussy. Someday, you'll look back and know you missed out on the greatest thing ever because you were a self-absorbed, controlling asshole."

Keith laughs and grabs his stomach. "My only regret is not dumping your prude ass sooner."

"What's going on?" Suzy asks, sneaking up behind us.

We both jump.

"Be quiet," Izzy whispers. "She's dumping Keith."

"Finally," Suzy mutters. "I hate that prick."

Keith smirks. "I mean, I still banged all the chicks I wanted, but it would've been easier without your lame ass clinging on me twenty-four seven."

Gigi touches her chest and moves toward him, but he moves away. "I was the clinger?" She pauses. "You're shitting me, right?" Her voice is louder now, and her anger's back. "Say that again, Keith. I dare you!"

Suzy grabs my arm and is holding so tight, I know I'm going to have a bruise tomorrow. "Oh God," she whispers.

Keith narrows his eyes, and his top lip curls. "You were a clingy bitch."

Right before my eyes, Gigi turns into the Karate Kid, kicking the kid right in the balls like she's done it a hundred times. He goes down like a sack of potatoes, holding his crotch and rolling on the ground, howling.

"I hope you enjoy fucking Amber tonight with a broken dick, motherfucker," she hisses as she stands over his body.

"I'm going to pretend I didn't hear any of this," Suzy says, and she's shuffling her feet like she doesn't know which way to move.

I know everyone talks about Izzy and how she's South Side through and through, but I think Gigi could give her a run for her money. The girl is fearless and had no problem taking down a man larger than her.

"I taught her well," Izzy says with a smile on her face. "Run." She shoos us as Gigi starts to move away from Keith, leaving him on the ground flailing around like an idiot.

He sounds like a wounded animal the way he's carrying on. I think the kick she got in will make it damn near impossible for that boy to get any action from Amber or anyone for a long, long time.

The three of us walk quickly across the backyard, making our way to the buffet table, pretending to be interested in the food.

"Hey," Gigi says, but there's no anger in her voice. "I'm starving." She plucks a tiny quiche off the table and shoves it into her mouth. "This is so good," she moans, closing her eyes.

I'm gawking at her; I can't help myself. I just saw this little girl take down a man, and now she's eating mini quiches and acting like nothing happened.

"Is something on my face?" she asks with her mouth full, staring at the three of us.

"No. Why, baby?" Suzy asks.

"You're all looking at me funny."

Izzy grabs a plate, trying to keep her eyes off Gigi, but she's smiling. "We're just so happy. Today was such a big day for you."

"Bigger than you know," Gigi says as she grabs more quiches, placing them in the palm of the same hand that slapped Keith right across his face.

That little bastard deserved everything she gave him. He deserved worse, actually. If Joe would've heard the names that boy called his daughter, Keith wouldn't still be breathing.

Gigi stares at her mother. "Ma, you're freaking me out."

Suzy grabs her daughter and hugs her tight. "I'm just so proud of you, Gigi. So, so proud."

Gigi hugs her back with one arm because her other hand still has the quiches. "It's only high school graduation, Ma. It's not that big of a deal. It's not like I cured cancer or anything."

Suzy's eyes glisten in the sunlight as she pulls away. "I know." Her face contorts into a painful smile as she tries to hold back the tears.

"Let's go check out the dessert table, kid," Izzy says and starts to usher Gigi away. "Your mother needs some time to compose herself."

"She's always a little crazy, Auntie." Gigi laughs and pops another quiche into her mouth.

"Was I that bad?" Suzy asks me.

I shrug. "No. You weren't bad. I would've been worse." I haven't moved or spoken much, still shell-shocked from everything that happened.

"Mommy. Mommy." Tate runs across the yard, holding a cupcake in each hand. "They have cupcakes here." She smiles, holding them up to show me.

"Don't eat too many, baby, or you'll get a tummy ache," I tell her.

She shakes her head. "I promise," she lies.

This girl is like a bottomless pit, and I know no matter what she says, the food's going to win out over her will.

"I'm going to show Daddy." And like that, she's off to the other side of the yard.

"Enjoy this age," Suzy tells me, blotting the tears away from her eyes. "Soon she'll be kicking her own Keith in the balls."

I stare at her for a moment before bursting into laughter. I can see it. One hundred percent can I see that cupcake-loving little girl kneeing some asshole right in his crotch for treating her badly.

Little girls learn how they're supposed to be loved from their father. With the way Angelo is with Tate, I have no doubt she'll know her worth and won't put up with any man's shit, especially a low-life loser life Keith.

"As long as she learns to fight like Gigi, I think everything will turn out just fine," I tell Suzy and interlock our arms. "I think we could both use a glass of wine." I smile.

She laughs. "Today is a day to celebrate. My little girl is single and finished with high school."

"Now it's time for college."

Suzy stops walking. "Oh God, I don't even want to think of her with college boys."

"Sweetheart, I think she can handle herself just fine. She had all these men—" I wave my other hand around the yard "—showing her how to protect herself, and she has a good head on her shoulders. I think she'll do just fine at college."

Suzy nods and finally takes a step. "You're right. My girl can really kick some butt, huh?"

"She's a Gallo." I smile.

That means something. It means more than I ever knew when I first started dating Angelo. They aren't just a family. They're a way of being.

Proud.

Strong.

Defiant.

Dominant.

Fearless.

Loyal.

I am a part of something greater than I have ever been in my entire life.

EPILOGUE

ANGELO

Lucio leans back and looks around the bar. "Do you think we should move?" he asks.

My eyes follow his, soaking in everything we've built together. Sure, my parents opened the bar, but since we've taken it over, the place has thrived. I no longer think of Hook & Hustle as theirs, because now, it's ours. "I don't know what the right answer is, Luc."

Daphne takes a sip of her whiskey before she lets out a long, exasperated sigh. "Chicago is in my blood. This is home to me. If you guys want to head south, you can, but I'm not ready to give up the dirt and grit of the city yet. Plus, they have shit pizza down there and no good bakeries. There's no Chinatown, no Greektown, and did I mention the pizza is shit?"

"Twice." I smile.

"I still have two years on my contract." Vinnie shrugs. "And Bianca's family is here. I can't ask her to leave them so I can be warm. And her father would have my balls if I took away his princess and our baby girl. I can't do that to the man."

Lucio refills everyone's glasses. "True, but we could buy a kick-ass vacation house down there. We could use more time off, especially with the kids. With Ma and Pop doing the snowbird shit, we have plenty of reasons to go there in the winter and escape the snow."

"That's an idea I can get behind," Daphne says. "I can't give this up." She looks around before lifting the glass to her lips.

"This? The bar?" I ask, staring at my beautiful sister.

"This," she says as she waves her hands in front of her, toward us, and almost spilling her drink. "Us."

I smile because I couldn't imagine not having *this* either. Hook & Hustle isn't just a bar or our business; it's about family and what we built together. There's not a day that goes by when I don't see my brothers and sister. Hell, we grew up in this place. It's just as much our home as walking through the front door of our parents' place upstairs.

"I want our kids to know what *this* feels like too.

It's important that they're close, more like siblings than cousins."

"They already are," Daphne says. "And I know the weather here sucks and the city isn't the safest place, but it's home and will always be home."

Tilly comes through the front door and heads through the crowd to our table. "I'm sorry I'm late," she says and leans down to kiss my cheek.

"Babe," I say, grabbing her wrist before she has a chance to sit. "How about a real kiss?"

She rolls her eyes but gives me what I've been waiting hours to get. "Where's everybody else?" she asks as she shrugs off her coat.

"They're coming. The roads are a mess, so they're stuck in traffic."

"There're at least eight inches covering the sidewalk, and no one was prepared for something this big."

"That's what she said," Lucio adds with a laugh.

"You're an idiot, and anyway—" Daphne smirks "— eight inches isn't all that impressive."

His eyes darken. "I don't want to hear about your sex life, Daphne."

"We're here." Bianca appears beside our table with Delilah. "Shit is crazy out there."

Delilah and Bianca both give their men kisses before sitting down with us. The only person missing is

Leo, but he's at the hotel, unable to get away with the freak spring blizzard.

"Maybe I should go check on the kids," Delilah says almost before she has her coat off.

"They're fine, baby. Christine is watching them, and they're playing."

Since our parents are out of town until spring, we've hired a babysitter—who's more like a nanny—to take care of the kids upstairs while we work. It allows us to keep them close and together while we work.

"Thank God for her," Delilah says.

I throw my arm around the back of Tilly's chair and pull her closer. "You good, sweet?"

"I couldn't be better," she says with the biggest smile. "What's not to be happy about? I've got a good man, an amazing family, and all the love in the world."

She's right. It doesn't matter that it's cold outside and the snow is falling so fast, soon the roads will be undrivable. All that matters is that I have everything I ever wanted.

I'm as rich as they come. Not just in wealth, but in love. A man is nothing without his family, the love of a good woman, and healthy children.

The road to get here wasn't pretty, but in the end, my soul is settled. My heart is full. And time keeps moving while I soak up all the goodness that is life.

Do you love the Gallos?

There's more sexy, sweet family fun in the **NEW Men of Inked: Heatwave** series!

This is the Gallos NEXT GENERATION!

Features City & Suzy's daughter (Throttle Me) visit *menofinked.com/flame* and get your copy of Flame.

Visit *menofinked.com/flame* to learn more about **FLAME** and the NEW Men of Inked: Heatwave series.

Haven't met the other side of the Gallo Family?

Visit *menofinked.com/free* to download your FREE copy now!

Visit menofinked.com to sign up for my VIP newsletter, featuring exclusive eBooks, special deals, and giveaways!

or

text **BLISS** to **24587**

to sign up for VIP text news

There's other ways to follow me...
BookBub | Twitter | Facebook | Instagram

I'd love to hear from you.

www.menofinked.com

Join my PRIVATE Facebook Reader Group

ABOUT THE AUTHOR

Chelle Bliss is the *Wall Street Journal* and *USA Today* bestselling author of Men of Inked: Southside Series, Misadventures of a City Girl, the Men of Inked, and ALFA Investigations series.

She hails from the Midwest, but currently lives near the beach even though she hates sand. She's a full-time writer, time-waster extraordinaire, social media addict, coffee fiend, and ex history teacher.

She loves spending time with her two cats, alpha boyfriend, and chatting with readers. To learn more about Chelle, please visit menofinked.com or chellebliss.com.

JOIN MY NEWSLETTER
by visiting *menofinked.com*

Text Notifications (US only)
➜ Text **BLISS** to **24587**

WHERE TO FOLLOW CHELLE:

WEBSITE | TWITTER | FACEBOOK |
INSTAGRAM
JOIN MY PRIVATE FACEBOOK GROUP

Want to drop me a line?
authorchellebliss@gmail.com
www.chellebliss.com

f facebook.com/authorchellebliss 1

BB bookbub.com/authors/chelle-bliss

O instagram.com/authorchellebliss

🐦 twitter.com/ChelleBliss 1

www.chellebliss.com

CHELLE BLISS

USA TODAY BESTSELLING AUTHOR

MEN OF INKED SERIES

"One of the sexiest series of all-time"

-Bookbub Reviewers

Download book 1 for FREE!

- Book 1 - Throttle Me (Joe aka City)
- Book 2 - Hook Me (Mike)
- Book 3 - Resist Me (Izzy)
- Book 4 - Uncover Me (Thomas)
- Book 5 - Without Me (Anthony)
- Book 6 - Honor Me (City)
- Book 7 - Worship Me (Izzy)

ALFA INVESTIGATIONS SERIES

Wickedly hot alphas with tons of heart pounding suspense!

- Book 1 - Sinful Intent (Morgan)
- Book 2 - Unlawful Desire (Frisco)
- Book 3 - Wicked Impulse (Bear)
- Book 4 - Guilty Sin (Ret)

MEN OF INKED: SOUTHSIDE SERIES

Join the Chicago Gallo Family with their strong alphas, sassy women, and tons of fun.

- Book 1 - Maneuver (Lucio)
- Book 2 - Flow (Daphne)
- Book 3 - Hook (Angelo)
- Book 4 - Hustle (Vinnie)
- Book 5 - Love (Angelo)

SINGLE READS

- Mend
- Enshrine
- Misadventures of a City Girl
- Misadventures with a Speed Demon
- Rebound (Flash aka Sam)
- Top Bottom Switch (Ret)

NAILED DOWN SERIES

- Book 1 - Nailed Down
- Book 2 - Tied Down
- Book 3 - Kneel Down

TAKEOVER DUET

What happens when you sleep with your biggest enemy?

- Book 1 - Acquisition
- Book 2 - Merger

FILTHY SERIES

- Dirty Work
- Dirty Secret
- Dirty Defiance

LOVE AT LAST SERIES

- Book 1 - Untangle Me
- Book 2 - Kayden

BOX SETS & COLLECTIONS

- Men of Inked Volume 1
- Men of Inked Volume 2
- Love at Last Series
- ALFA Investigations Series
- Filthy Series
- Takeover Duet

**View Chelle's entire collection of books at
menofinked.com/books**

To learn more about Chelle's books visit *menofinked.com* or *chellebliss.com*

ACKNOWLEDGMENTS

There are dozens of people who help me in the creation and inspiration for a new book. I hadn't planned on writing a fifth book, but you—my dear reader—asked for more and I couldn't say no.

Who doesn't love to spend more time with the Gallos? Not me. I love their world. The love. The loyalty. The family. Everything about them makes me smile. They're my happy place and escape.

To my lovely betas and friends... thank you for always being there. I know I'm not easy and I change things so quickly sometimes I give you whiplash. I'm sorry, but thanks for not giving up on me.

To my editor, Lisa, thanks for putting up with my insanity. I know I drive you crazy and my grammar is shit most times, but I try. I know my tenses will forever be fucked, but you've accepted my imperfections and have learned to roll with them.

To my proofreader and eagle eyes, Julie, thanks for always being quick and loving my words. You always find the little things that slip through the cracks. Plus, you save me from having to read over the book so many times my eyes almost start to bleed.

To my guy, Brian, thanks for putting up with my craziness and giving me time to write. I know it's not easy, but you do it anyway. Thank you for taking care of me, cooking, cleaning, helping with the business, and everything else you do so I can write all the words.

To my readers... thank you loving my books. The way you've embraced the Gallos in the Men of Inked has blown me away. I'll live in this world as long as you're willing to devour the books and claim the men as your own.

CPSIA information can be obtained
at www.ICGtesting.com
Printed in the USA
BVHW032154040819
555074BV00001B/5/P